"I am used to the crack of leathery dragon wings in the sweet, sharp air of the early dawn. I am used to the sound of red battle, the drumming of hooves on bloody earth, the screams of the dying, the yells of the victorious. I am used to warring against demons and monsters, sorcerers and ghouls. I have sailed on magic ships and fought hand to hand with reptilian savages. I have encountered the Jade Man himself. I have fought side by side with the elementals, who are my allies. I have battled black evil...."

MICHAEL MOORCOCK
in DAW Books includes:

THE JEWEL IN THE SKULL
THE MAD GOD'S AMULET
THE SWORD OF THE DAWN
THE RUNESTAFF

ELRIC
at the
End of Time

MICHAEL MOORCOCK

DAW BOOKS, INC.
DONALD A. WOLLHEIM, PUBLISHER

1633 Broadway, New York, NY 10019

First DAW Printing, May 1985

5   6   7   8   9

PRINTED IN THE U.S.A.

CONTENTS

For Lemmy.
For Pete Green, wherever you are
now. For Alex Harvey, much lamented.
And for all those other old farts
of musicians who, as Martin Stone
reports, nowadays jump out of the
bus and head for the nearest second-hand
bookshop . . .

Introduction

ELRIC AT THE END OF TIME was the last story I wrote about the albino prince. In some ways it's an affectionate commentary on the kind of fantasy hero with whom I'm most closely identified and it's also based on the remark made some years ago by M. John Harrison that the people who inhabit my End of Time stories might, from Elric's perspective, seem to be the very Lords of Chaos themselves. The story brings together elements from most of the series which, by the mid-seventies, I was completing. It was finished in 1977, originally for a book which Big O intended to publish and which Rodney Matthews would illustrate. Big O effectively folded before the book could appear. The Rodney Matthews paintings all exist, but only a few of them have been seen (principally in Rodney's own 1983 Calendar) which is a great pity, since they represent some of his best and most ambitious work. The only previous appearance of the story was in Terri Windling's and Mark Arnold's *Elsewhere* anthology, which came out in the USA in 1981.

The Last Enchantment was meant to be the final

Elric story. It was written in 1962, only a short while after the first had appeared in magazine form and before I wrote what was to become *Stormbringer*. I gave the story to Ted Carnell for his magazine *Science Fantasy* but he didn't want a "last" Elric story. He persuaded me to write some more novellas and in his capacity as my agent sent *The Last Enchantment* to America, where it was rejected. Some fifteen years later Ted's successor, Les Flood, came across the story and returned it to me. It eventually appeared in *Ariel* magazine in the U.S. in 1978, illustrated by Tim Conrad. That was its only publication until now. Like *Elric at the End of Time* it has never been published in England and this is its first appearance in book form.

The *Sojan* stories are my first fantasy tales to be professionally published. They were begun in the 1950s for *Tarzan Adventures*, before I came to edit the magazine. I was seventeen when they started to appear and they were not published in book form until Dave Britton and Mike Butterworth republished them as *Sojan*, the first book they did as Savoy Editions. It was re-illustrated by Jim Cawthorn, the original illustrator who has worked with me through my whole career as a writer of fantastic fiction. This book was primarily a compendium of my earliest work, together with some of my writing about my own fiction and I have included one or two other pieces from *Sojan* here.

The Stone Thing was written in response to a request from Eric Bentcliffe, editor of the fanzine *Triode*, which I used to write for in the fifties. It is one of several parodies of my own work which I've done over the years (some of which, it could be argued, were not published as such) and it's one I'm particularly fond of. *Triode* specialised in humorous "fan fiction"—stories written about actual personalities in the SF field—and dates from the period in which science fiction fans did not take themselves quite so seriously as nowadays, and those who made religion from an enthusiasm were generally mocked for it. I hope the story itself will show some readers that I am neither in touch with secret supernatural forces nor the spokesman for an illuminating new mystical knowledge. As a matter of fact I'm by nature extraordinarily sceptical of the supernatural. I have always conceived my fantastic stories simply as that—fantastic stories, escapist entertainment which hopes to give some pleasure to the reader. Any profundities in those romances are a tribute to the one who discovers them rather than to me. For a long while the exaggerated reaction of some readers to my fantasies caused me to try to dismiss them altogether. However, I should like to say that I denigrate neither the stories nor their readers, though I do prefer my comedies to my melodramas and personally would put a greater value on books such as *Gloriana, The Condition of Muzak, Byzantium Endures* or *The Brothel in Rosenstrasse*. I've always had a happy facility for fantasy and I suppose it's common enough for someone to make less of something which comes easily to them.

Some of the non-fiction pieces about Elric and Co. which were in the original Sojan selection edited by Dave Britton are still here, for whatever interest they provide. I have Dave Britton and Mike Butterworth to thank for many things, not least their willingness to sift through long-forgotten piles of paper and find manuscripts and tear-sheets (*The Golden Barge* would never have been published had it not been for their retaining a copy of the manuscript which I had thought permanently lost) and I should also like to recognise, once again, Ted Carnell's encouragement as the editor of my first Elric stories, Peter Ledeboer's kindness as the publisher who originally commissioned the title story as a vehicle for Rodney Matthew's illustrations, the present publishers Alison Peacock, Simon Scott and Nick Webb of NEL and the encouragement, inspiration and friendship of many people, amongst them Jim Cawthorn, Eric Bentcliffe, Ron Bennett, Alan Dodd, Arthur Thomson and Ethel Lindsay who have known me since, as an enthusiastic and, I'm sure, sometimes irritating fifteen-year-old, I first began to write the Sojan stories.

Michael Moorcock,
Fulham Road
July 1983

ELRIC

Elric at the End of Time

1. In Which Mrs. Persson Detects An Above Average Degree of Chaos In The Megaflow

RETURNING FROM China to London and the Spring of 1936, Una Persson found an unfamiliar quality of pathos in most of the friends she had last seen, as far as she recalled, during the Blitz on her way back from 1970. Then they had been desperately hearty: it was a comfort to understand that the condition was not permanent. Here, at present, Pierrot ruled and she felt she possessed a better grip on her power. This was, she admitted with shame, her favourite moral climate for it encouraged in her an enormously gratifying sense of spiritual superiority: the advantage of having been born, originally, into a later and probably more sophisticated age. The 1960s. Some women, she reflected, were forced to have children in order to enjoy this pleasure.

But she was uneasy, so she reported to the local Time Centre and the bearded, sullen features of Sergeant Alvarez who welcomed her in white, apologising for the fact that he had himself only just that

15

morning left the Lower Devonian and had not had time to change.

"It's the megaflow, as you guessed," he told her, operating toggles to reveal his crazy display systems. "We've lost control."

"We never really had it." She lit a Sherman's and shook her long hair back over the headrest of the swivel chair, opening her military overcoat and loosening her webbing. "Is it worse than usual?"

"Much." He sipped cold coffee from his battered silver mug. "It cuts through every plane we can pick up—a rogue current swerving through the dimensions. Something of a twister."

"Jerry?"

"He's dormant. We checked. But it's like him, certainly. Most probably another aspect."

"Oh, sod." Una straightened her shoulders.

"That's what I thought," said Alvarez. "Someone's going to have to do a spot of rubato." He studied a screen. It was Greek to Una. For a moment a pattern formed. Alvarez made a note. "Yes. It can either be fixed at the nadir or the zenith. It's too late to try anywhere in between. I think it's up to you, Mrs. P."

She got to her feet. "Where's the zenith?"

"The End of Time."

"Well," she said, "that's something."

She opened her bag and made sure of her jar of instant coffee. It was the one thing she couldn't get at the End of Time.

"Sorry," said Alvarez, glad that the expert had been there and that he could remain behind.

"It's just as well," she said. "This period's no good for my moral well-being. I'll be off, then."

"Someone's got to." Alvarez failed to seem sympathetic. "It's Chaos out there."

"You don't have to tell me."

She entered the make-shift chamber and was on her way to the End of Time.

2. In Which The Eternal Champion Finds Himself at the End of Time

ELRIC OF MELNIBONÉ shook a bone-white fist at the greedy, glaring stars—the eyes of all those men whose souls he had stolen to sustain his own enfeebled body. He looked down. Though it seemed he stood on something solid, there was only more blackness falling away below him. It was as if he hung at the centre of the universe. And here, too, were staring points of yellow light. Was he to be judged?

His half-sentient runesword, Stormbringer, in its scabbard on his left hip, murmured like a nervous dog.

He had been on his way to Imrryr, to his home, to reclaim his kingdom from his cousin Yyrkoon; sailing from the Isle of the Purple Towns where he had guested with Count Smiorgan Baldhead. Magic winds had caught the Filkharian trader as she crossed the unnamed water between the Vilmirian peninsula and the Isle of Melniboné. She had been borne into the Dragon Sea and thence to The Sorcerer's Isle, so-called because that barren place had once been the home of Cran Liret, the Thief of Spells, a wizard infamous for his borrowings, who had, at length, been dispatched by those he sought to rival. But much residual magic had been left behind. Certain spells had come into the keeping of the Krettii, a tribe of near-brutes who had migrated to the island from the region of The Silent Land less than fifty years before. Their shaman, one Grrodd Ybene Eenr, had made unthinking use of devices buried by the dying sorcerer as the spells of his peers sucked life and sanity from them. Elric had dealt with more than one clever wizard, but never with so mindless a power. His battle had been long and exhausting and had required the sacrifice of most of the Filkharians as well as the entire tribe of Krettii. His sorcery had become increasingingly desperate. Sprite fought sprite, devil fell upon devil, in planes both physical and astral, all around the region of The Sorcerer's Isle. Eventually Elric had mounted a massive summoning against the allies of Grrodd Ybene Eenr with the result that the shaman had been at last overwhelmed and his remains scattered in Limbo. But Elric, captured by his own monstrous magickings, had followed his enemy and now he stood in the Void, crying out into appalling silence, hearing his words only in his skull:

"Arioch! Arioch! Aid me!"

But his patron Duke of Hell was absent. He could not exist here. He could not, for once, even hear his favourite protégé.

"Arioch! Repay my loyalty! I have given you blood and souls!"

He did not breathe. His heart had stopped. All his movements were sluggish.

The eyes looked down at him. They looked up at him. Were they glad? Did they rejoice in his terror?

"Arioch!"

He yearned for a reply. He would have wept, but no tears would come. His body was cold; less than dead, yet not alive. A fear was in him greater than any fear he had known before.

"Oh, Arioch! Aid me!"

He forced his right hand towards the pulsing pommel of Stormbringer which, alone, still possessed energy. The hilt of the sword was warm to his touch and, as slowly he folded his fingers around it, it seemed to swell in his fist and propel his arm upwards so that he did not draw the sword. Rather the sword forced his limbs into motion. And now it challenged the void, glowing with black fire, singing its high, gleeful battlesong.

"Our destinies are intertwined, Stormbringer," said Elric. "Bring us from this place, or those destinies shall never be fulfilled."

Stormbringer swung like the needle of a compass and Elric's unfeeling arm was wrenched round to go with it. In eight directions the sword swung, as if to the eight points of Chaos. It was questing—like a hound sniffing a trail. Then a yell sounded from within the strange metal of the blade; a distant cry of delight, it seemed to Elric. The sound one would hear if one stood above a valley listening to children playing far below.

Elric knew that Stormbringer had sensed a plane they might reach. Not necessarily their own, but one which would accept them. And, as a drowning mariner must yearn for the most inhospitable rock rather than no rock at all, Elric yearned for that plane.

"Stormbringer. Take us there."

The sword hesitated. It moaned. It was suspicious.

"Take us there!" whispered the albino to his runesword.

The sword struck back and forth, up and down, as if it battled invisible enemies. Elric scarcely kept his grip on it. It seemed that Stormbringer was frightened of the world it had detected and sought to drive it back but the act of seeking had in itself set them both in motion. Already Elric could feel himself being drawn through the darkness, towards something he could see very dimly beyond the myriad eyes, as dawn reveals clouds undetected in the night sky.

Elric thought he saw the shapes of crags, pointed and crazy. He thought he saw water, flat and ice-blue. The stars faded and there was snow beneath his feet, mountains all around him, a huge, blazing sun overhead—and above that another landscape, a desert, as a magic mirror might reflect the contrasting character of he who peered into it—a desert, quite as real as the snowy peaks in which he crouched, sword in hand, waiting for one of these landscapes to fade so that he might establish, to a degree, his bearings. Evidently the two planes had intersected.

But the landscape overhead did not fade. He could look up and see sand, mountains, vegetation, a sky which met his own sky at a point half-way along the curve of the huge sun—and blended with it. He looked about him. Snowy peaks in all directions. Above—desert everywhere. He felt dizzy, found that he was staring downward, reaching to cup some of the snow in his hand. It was ordinary snow, though it seemed reluctant to melt in contact with his flesh.

"This is a world of Chaos," he muttered. "It obeys no natural laws." His voice seemed loud, amplified by the peaks, perhaps. "That is why you did not want to come here. This is the world of powerful rivals."

Stormbringer was silent, as if all its energy were spent. But Elric did not sheath the blade. He began to trudge through the snow toward what seemed to be an abyss. Every so often he glanced upward, but the desert overhead had not faded, sun and sky remained the same. He wondered if he walked around the surface of a miniature world. That if he continued to go forward he might eventually reach the point where the two landscapes met. He wondered if this were not some punishment wished upon him by his untrustworthy allies of Chaos. Perhaps he must choose between death in the snow or death in the desert. He reached the edge of the abyss and looked down.

The walls of the abyss fell for all of five feet before reaching a floor of gold and silver squares which stretched for perhaps another seven feet before they reached the far wall, where the landscape continued— snow and crags—uninterrupted.

"This is undoubtedly where Chaos rules," said the Prince of Melniboné. He studied the smooth, chequered floor. It reflected parts of the snowy terrain and the desert world above it. It reflected the crimson-eyed albino who peered down at it, his features drawn in bewilderment and tiredness.

"I am at their mercy," said Elric. "They play with me. But I shall resist them, even as they destroy me." And some of his wild, careless spirit came back to him as he prepared to lower himself onto the chequered floor and cross to the opposite bank.

He was half-way over when he heard a grunting sound in the distance and a beast appeared, its paws slithering uncertainly on the smooth surface, its seven savage eyes glaring in all directions as if it sought the instigator of its terrible indignity.

And, at last, all seven eyes focused on Elric and the beast opened a mouth in which row upon row of thin, vicious teeth were arranged, and uttered a growl of unmistakable resentment.

Elric raised his sword. "Back, creature of Chaos. You threaten the Prince of Melniboné."

The beast was already propelling itself towards him. Elric flung his body to one side, aiming a blow with the sword as he did so, succeeding only in making a thin incision in the monster's heavily muscled hind leg. It shrieked and began to turn.

"Back."

Elric's voice was the brave, thin squeak of a lemming attacked by a hawk. He drove at the thing's snout with Stormbringer. The sword was heavy. It had spent all its energy and there was no more to give. Elric wondered why he, himself, did not weaken. Possibly the laws of nature were entirely abolished in the Realm of Chaos. He struck and drew blood. The beast paused, more in astonishment than fear.

Then it opened its jaws, pushed its back legs against the snowy bank, and shot towards the albino who tried to dodge it, lost his footing, and fell, sprawling backwards, on the gold and silver surface.

3. In Which Una Persson Discovers An Unexpected Snag

THE GIGANTIC beetle, rainbow carapace glittering, turned as if into the wind, which blew from the distant mountains, its thick, flashing wings beating rapidly as it bore its single passenger over the queer landscape.

On its back Mrs. Persson checked the instruments on her wrist. Ever since Man had begun to travel in time it had become necessary for the League to develop techniques to compensate for the fluctuations and disruptions in the spacetime continua; perpetually monitoring the chronoflow and megaflow. She pursed her lips. She had picked up the signal. She made the semi-sentient beetle swing a degree or two SSE and head directly for the mountains. She was in some sort of enclosed (but vast) environment. These mountains, as well as everything surrounding them, lay in the territory most utilised by the gloomy, natural-born Werther de Goethe, poet and romantic, solitary seeker after truth in a world no longer differentiating between the degrees of reality. He would not remember her, she knew, because, as far as Werther was concerned, they had not met yet. He had not even, if Una were correct, experienced his adventure with Mistress Christia, the Everlasting Concubine. A story on which she had dined out more than once, in duller eras.

The mountains drew closer. From here it was possible to see the entire arrangement (a creation of Werther's very much in character): a desert landscape, a central sun, and, inverted above it, winter mountains. Werther strove to make statements, like so many naïve artists before him, by presenting simple contrasts: The World is Bleak/The World is Cold/Barren Am I As I Grow Old/Tomorrow I Die, Entombed in Cold/For Silver My Poor Soul Was Sold— she remembered he was perhaps the worst poet she had encountered in an eternity of meetings with bad poets. He had taught himself to read and write in old, old English so that he might carve those words on one of his many abandoned tombs (half his time was spent in composing obituaries for himself). Like so many others he seemed to equate self-pity with artistic inspiration. In an earlier age he might have discovered his public and become quite rich (self-pity passing for passion in the popular understanding). Sometimes she regretted the passing of Wheldrake, so long ago, so far away, in a universe bearing scarcely any resemblances to those in which she normally operated.

She brought her wavering mind back to the problem. The beetle dipped and circled over the desert, but there was no sight of her quarry.

She was about to abandon the search when she heard a faint roaring overhead and she looked up to see another characteristic motif of Werther's—a gold and silver chessboard on which, upside down, a monstrous dog-like creature was bearing down on a tiny white-haired man dressed in the most abominable taste Una had seen for some time.

She directed the aircar upwards and then, reversing the machine as she entered the opposing gravity, downwards to where the barbarically costumed swordsman was about to be eaten by the beast.

"Shoo!" cried Una commandingly.

The beast raised a befuddled head.

"Shoo."

It licked lips and returned its seven-eyed gaze to the albino, who was now on his knees, using his large sword to steady himself as he climbed to his feet.

The jaws opened wider and wider. The pale man prepared, shakily, to defend himself.

Una directed the aircar at the beast's unkempt head. The great beetle connected with a loud crack. The monster's eyes widened in dismay. It yelped. It sat on its haunches and began to slide away, its claws making an unpleasant noise on the gold and silver tiles.

Una landed the aircar and gestured for the stranger to enter. She noticed with distaste that he was a somewhat unhealthy looking albino with gaunt features, exaggeratedly large and slanting eyes, ears that were virtually pointed, and glaring, half-mad red pupils.

And yet, undoubtedly, it was her quarry and there was nothing for it but to be polite.

"Do, please, get in," she said. "I am here to rescue you."

"*Shaarmraaam torjistoo quellahm vyeearrr,*" said the stranger in an accent that seemed to Una to be vaguely Scottish.

"Damn," she said, "that's all we need." She had been anxious to approach the albino in private, before one of the denizens of the End of Time could arrive and select him for a menagerie, but now she regretted that Werther or perhaps Lord Jagged were not here, for she realised that she needed one of their translation pills, those tiny tablets which could "engineer" the brain to understand a new language. By a fluke—or perhaps because of her presence here so often—the people at the End of Time currently spoke formal early twentieth-century English.

The albino—who wore a kind of tartan divided kilt, knee-length boots, a blue and white jerkin, a green cloak and a silver breastplate, with a variety of leather belts and metal buckles here and there upon his person—was vehemently refusing her offer of a lift. He raised the sword before him as he backed away, slipped once, reached the bank, scrambled through snow and disappeared behind a rock.

Mrs. Persson sighed and put the car into motion again.

4. In Which The Prince of Melniboné Encounters Further Terrors

XIOMBARG HERSELF, thought Elric as he slid beneath the snows into the cave. Well, he would have no dealings with the Queen of Chaos; not until he was forced to do so.

The cave was large. In the thin light from the gap above his head he could not see far. He wondered whether to return to the surface or risk going deeper into the cave. There was always the hope that he would find another way out. He was attempting to recall some rune that would aid him, but all he knew depended either upon the aid of elementals who did not exist on this plane, or upon the Lords of Chaos themselves—and they were unlikely to come to his assistance in their own Realm. He was marooned here: the single mouse in a world of cats.

Almost unconsciously he found himself moving downwards, realising that the cave had become a tunnel. He was feeling hungry but, apart from the monster and the woman in the magical carriage, had seen no sign of life. Even the cavern did not seem entirely natural.

It widened; there was phosphorescent light. He realised that the walls were of transparent crystal and, behind the walls, were all manner of artefacts. He saw crowns, sceptres and chains of precious jewels; cabinets of complicated carving; weapons of strangely turned metal; armour, clothing, things whose use he could not guess—and food. There were sweetmeats, fruits, flans and pies, all out of reach.

Elric groaned. This was torment. Perhaps deliberately planned torment. A thousand voices whispered to him in a beautiful, alien language: *"Bie-meee . . . Bie-meee . . ."* the voices murmured. *"Baa-gen baa-gen . . ."*

They seemed to be promising every delight, if only he could pass through the walls; but they were of transparent quartz, lit from within. He raised Stormbringer, half-tempted to try to break down the barrier, but he knew that even his sword was, at its most powerful, incapable of destroying the magic of Chaos.

He paused, gaping with astonishment at a group of small dogs which looked at him with large brown eyes, tongues lolling, and jumped up at him.

"O, Nee Tubbens!" intoned one of the voices.

"Gods." screamed Elric. "This torture is too much!" He swung his body this way and that, threatening with his sword, but the voices continued to murmur and promise, displaying their riches but never allowing him to touch.

The albino panted. His crimson eyes glared about him. "You would drive me insane, eh? Well, Elric of Melniboné has witnessed more frightful threats than this. You will need to do more if you would destroy his mind!"

And he ran through the whispering passages, looking to neither his right nor his left, until, quite suddenly, he had run into blazing daylight and stood staring down into pale infinity—a blue and endless void.

He looked up. And he screamed.

Overhead were the gentle hills and dales of a rural landscape, with rivers, grazing cattle, woods and cottages. He expected to fall, headlong, but he did not. He was on the brink of the abyss. The cliff-face of red sandstone fell immediately below and then was the tranquil void. He looked back: "Baa-gen . . . O, Nee Tubbens . . ."

A bitter smile played about the albino's bloodless lips as, decisively, he sheathed his sword.

"Well, then," he said. "Let them do their worst!"

And, laughing, he launched himself over the brink of the cliff.

5. In Which Werther de Goethe Makes A Wonderful Discovery

WITH A gesture of quiet pride, Werther de Goethe indicated his gigantic skull.

"It is very large, Werther," said Mistress Christia, the Everlasting Concubine, turning a power ring to adjust the shade of her eyes so that they perfectly matched the day.

"It is monstrous," said Werther modestly. "It reminds us all of the Inevitable Night."

"Who was that?" enquired golden-haired Gaf the Horse in Tears, at present studying ancient legendry. "Sir Lew Grady?"

"I mean Death," Werther told him, "which overwhelms us all."

"Well, not us," pointed out the Duke of Queens, as usual a trifle literal minded. "Because we're immortal, as you know."

Werther offered him a sad, pitying look and sighed briefly. "Retain your delusions, if you will."

Mistress Christia stroked the gloomy Werther's long, dark locks. "There, there," she said. "We have compensations, Werther."

"Without Death," intoned the Last Romantic, "there is no point to Life."

As usual, they could not follow him, but they nodded gravely and politely.

"The skull," continued Werther, stroking the side of his aircar (which was in the shape of a large flying reptile) to make it circle and head for the left eyesocket, "is a Symbol not only of our Morality, but also of our Fruitless Ambitions."

"Fruit?" Bishop Castle, drowsing at the rear of the vehicle, became interested. His hobby was currently orchards. "Less? My pine-trees, you know, are proving a problem. The apples are much smaller than I was led to believe."

"The skull is lovely," said Mistress Christia with valiant enthusiasm. "Well, now that we have seen it . . ."

"The outward shell," Werther told her. "It is what it hides which is more important. Man's Foolish Yearnings are all encompassed therein. His Greed, his Need for the Impossible, the Heat of his Passions, the Coldness which must Finally Overtake him. Through this eye-socket you will encounter a little invention of my own called The Bargain Basement of the Mind . . ."

He broke off in astonishment.

On the top edge of the eye-socket a tiny figure had emerged.

"What's that?" enquired the Duke of Queens, craning his head back. "A random thought?"

"It is not mine at all!"

The figure launched itself into the sky and seemed to fly, with flailing limbs, towards the sun.

Werther frowned, watching the tiny man disappear. "The gravity field is reversed there," he said absently, "in order to make the most of the paradox, you understand. There is a snowscape, a desert . . ." But he was much more interested in the newcomer. "How do you think he got into my skull?"

"At least he's enjoying himself. He seems to be laughing," Mistress Christia bent an ear towards the thin sound, which grew fainter and fainter at first, but became louder again. "He's coming back."

Werther nodded. "Yes. The field's no longer reversed." He touched a power ring.

The laughter stopped and became a yell of rage. The figure hurtled down on them. It had a sword in one white hand and its red eyes blazed.

Hastily, Werther stroked another ring. The stranger tumbled into the bottom of the aircar and lay there panting, cursing and groaning.

"How wonderful!" cried Werther. "Oh, this is a traveller from some rich, romantic past. Look at him! What else could he be? What a prize!"

The stranger rose to his feet and raised the sword high above his head, defying the amazed and delighted passengers as he screamed at the top of his voice:

"Heegeegrowinaz!"

"Good afternoon," said Mistress Christia. She reached in her purse for a translation pill and found one. "I wonder if you would care to swallow this— it's quite harmless . . ."

"Yakooom, oom glallio," said the albino contemptuously.

"Aha," said Mistress Christia. "Well, just as you please."

The Duke of Queens pointed towards the other socket. A huge, whirring beetle came sailing from it. In its back was someone he recognised with pleasure. "Mrs. Persson!"

Una brought her aircar alongside.

"Is he in your charge?" asked Werther with undisguised disappointment. "If so, I could offer you . . ."

"I'm afraid he means a lot to me," she said.

"From your own age?" Mistress Christia also recognised Una. She still offered the translation pill in the palm of her hand. "He seems a mite suspicious of us."

"I'd noticed," said Una. "It would be useful if he would accept the pill. However, if he will not, one of us . . ."

"I would be happy," offered the generous Duke of Queens. He tugged at his green and gold beard. "Werther de Goethe, Mrs. Persson."

"Perhaps I had better," said Una nodding to Werther. The only problem with translation pills was that they did their job so thoroughly. You could speak the language perfectly, but you could speak no other.

Werther was, for once, positive. "Let's all take a pill," he suggested.

Everyone at the End of Time carried translation pills, in case of meeting a visitor from Space or the Past.

Mistress Christia handed hers to Una and found another. They swallowed.

"Creatures of Chaos," said the newcomer with cool dignity, "I demand that you release me. You cannot hold a mortal in this way, not unless he has struck a bargain with you. And no bargain was struck which would bring me to the Realm of Chaos."

"It's actually more orderly than you'd think," said Werther apologetically. "Your first experience, you see, was the world of my skull, which was deliberately muddled. I meant to show what Confusion was the Mind of Man . . ."

"May I introduce Mistress Christia, the Everlasting Concubine," said the Duke of Queens, on his best manners. "This is Mrs. Persson, Bishop Castle, Gaf the Horse in Tears. Werther de Goethe—your unwitting host—and I am the Duke of Queens. We welcome you to our world. Your name, sir . . . ?"

"You must know me, my lord duke," said Elric.

"For I am Elric of Melniboné, Emperor by Right of Birth, Inheritor of the Ruby Throne, Bearer of the Actorios, Wielder of the Black Sword . . ."

"Indeed!" said Werther de Goethe. In a whispered aside to Mrs. Persson: "What a marvellous scowl! What a noble sneer!"

"You are an important personage in your world, then?" said Mistress Christia, fluttering the eyelashes she had just extended by half an inch. "Perhaps you would allow me . . ."

"I think he wishes to be returned to his home," said Mrs. Persson hastily.

"Returned?" Werther was astonished. "But the Morphail Effect! It is impossible."

"Not in this case, I think," she said. "For if he is not returned there is no telling the fluctuations which will take place throughout the dimensions . . ."

They could not follow her, but they accepted her tone.

"Aye," said Elric darkly, "return me to my realm, so that I may fulfill my own doom-laden destiny . . ."

Werther looked upon the albino with affectionate delight. "Aha! A fellow spirit! I, too, have a doom-laden destiny."

"I doubt it is as doom-laden as mine." Elric peered moodily back at the skull as the two aircars fled away towards a gentle horizon where exotic trees bloomed.

"Well," said Werther with an effort, "perhaps it is not, though I assure you . . ."

"I have looked upon hell-born horror," said Elric, "and communicated with the very Gods of the Uttermost Darkness. I have seen things which would turn other men's minds to useless jelly . . ."

"Jelly?" interrupted Bishop Castle. "Do you, in

your turn, have any expertise with, for instance, blackbird trees?''

"Your words are meaningless," Elric told him, glowering. "Why do you torment me so, my lords? I did not ask to visit your world. I belong in the world of men, in the Young Kingdoms, where I seek my weird. Why, I have but lately experienced adventures . . .''

"I do think we have one of those bores," murmured Bishop Castle to the Duke of Queens, "so common amongst time-travellers. They all believe themselves unique."

But the Duke of Queens refused to be drawn. He had developed a liking for the frowning albino. Gaf the Horse in Tears was also plainly impressed, for he had fashioned his own features into a rough likeness of Elric's. The Prince of Melniboné pretended insouciance, but it was evident to Una that he was frightened. She tried to calm him.

"People here at the End of Time . . ." she began.

"No soft words, my lady." A cynical smile played about the albino's lips. "I know you for that great unholy temptress, Queen of the Swords, Xiombarg herself."

"I assure you, I am as human as you, sir . . .''

"Human? I, human? I am not human, madam—though I be a mortal, 'tis true. I am of older blood, the blood of the Bright Empire itself, the blood of R'lin K'ren A'a which Cran Liret mocked, not understanding what it was he laughed at. Aye, though forced to summon aid from Chaos, I made no bargain to become a slave in your realm . . .''

"I assure you—um—your majesty," said Una, "that we had not meant to insult you and your presence here was no doing of ours. I am, as it happens, a stranger here myself. I came especially to see you, to help you escape . . .''

"Ha!" said the albino. "I have heard such words before. You would lure me into some worse trap than this. Tell me, where is Duke Arioch? He, at least, I owe some allegiance to."

"We have no one of that name," apologised Mistress Christia. She enquired of Gaf, who knew everyone. "No time-traveller?"

"None," Gaf studied Elric's eyes and made a small adjustment to his own. He sat back, satisfied.

Elric shuddered and turned away mumbling.

"You are very welcome here," said Werther. "I cannot tell you how glad I am to meet one as essentially morbid and self-pitying as myself!"

Elric did not seem flattered.

"What can we do to make you feel at home?" asked Mistress Christia. She had changed her hair to a rather glossy blue in the hope, perhaps, that Elric would find it more attractive. "Is there anything you need?"

"Need? Aye. Peace of mind. Knowledge of my true destiny. A quiet place where I can be with Cymoril, whom I love."

"What does this Cymoril look like?" Mistress Christia became just a trifle over-eager.

"She is the most beautiful creature in the universe," said Elric.

"It isn't very much to go on," said Mistress Christia. "If you could imagine a picture, perhaps? There are devices in the old cities which could visualise your thoughts. We could go there. I should be happy to fill in for her, as it were . . ."

"What? You offer me a simulacrum? Do you not think I should detect such witchery at once? Ah, this is loathsome! Slay me, if you will, or continue the torment. I'll listen no longer!"

They were floating now, between high cliffs. On a ledge far below a group of time-travellers pointed up at them. One waved desperately.

"You've offended him, Mistress Christia," said Werther pettishly. "You don't understand how sensitive he is."

"Yes I do." She was aggrieved. "I was only being sympathetic."

"Sympathy!" Elric rubbed at his long, somewhat pointed jaw. "Ha! What do I want with sympathy?"

"I never heard anyone who wanted it more." Mistress Christia was kind. "You're like a little boy, really, aren't you?"

"Compared to the ancient Lords of Chaos, I am a child, aye. But my blood is old and cold, the blood of decaying Melniboné, as well you know." And with a huge sigh the albino seated himself at the far end of the car and rested his head on his fist. "Well? What is your pleasure, my lords and ladies of Hell?"

"It is your pleasure we are anxious to achieve," Werther told him. "Is there anything at all we can do? Some environment we can manufacture? What are you used to?"

"Used to? I am used to the crack of leathery dragon wings in the sweet, sharp air of the early dawn. I am used to the sound of red battle, the drumming of hooves on bloody earth, the screams of the dying, the yells of the victorious. I am used to warring against demons and monsters, sorcerers and ghouls. I have sailed on magic ships and fought hand to hand with reptilian savages. I have encountered the Jade Man himself. I have fought side by side with the elementals, who are my allies. I have battled black evil . . .''

"Well," said Werther, "that's something to go on, at any rate. I'm sure we can . . .''

"Lord Elric won't be staying," began Una Persson politely. "You see—these fluctuations in the mega-flow—not to mention his own destiny . . . He should not be here, at all, Werther."

"Nonsense!" Werther flung a black velvet arm about the stiff shoulders of his new friend. "It is evident that our destinies are one. Lord Elric is as grief-haunted as myself!"

"How can you know what it is to be haunted by grief . . . ?" murmured the albino. His face was half-buried in Werther's generous sleeve.

Mrs. Persson controlled herself. She rose from Werther's aircar and made for her own. "Well," she said, "I must be off. I hope to see you later, everybody."

They sang out their farewells.

Una Persson turned her beetle westward, towards Castle Canaria, the home of her old friend Lord Jagged.

She needed help and advice.

6. In Which Elric of Melniboné Resists the Temptations of the Chaos Lords

ELRIC REFLECTED on the subtle way in which laughing Lords of Chaos had captured him. Apparently, he was merely a guest and quite free to wander where he would in their Realm. Actually, he was in their power as much as if they had chained him, for he could not flee this flying dragon and they had al-ready demonstrated their enormous magical gifts in subtle ways, primarily with their shapechanging. Only the one who called himself Werther de Goethe (plainly a leader in the hierarchy of Chaos) still had the face and clothing he had worn when first encountered.

It was evident that this realm obeyed no natural laws, that it was mutable according to the whims of its powerful inhabitants. They could destroy him with a breath and had, subtly enough, given him evidence of that fact. How could he possibly escape such danger? By calling upon the Lords of Law for aid? But he owed them no loyalty and they, doubtless, regarded him as their enemy. But if he were to transfer his allegiance to Law . . .

These thoughts and more continued to engage him, while his captors chatted easily in the ancient High Speech of Melniboné, itself a version of the very language of Chaos. It was one of the other ways in which they revealed themselves for what they were. He fingered his runesword, wondering if it would be possible to slay such a lord and steal his energy, giving himself enough power for a little while to hurl himself back to his own sphere . . .

The one called Lord Werther was leaning over the side of the beast-vessel. "Oh, come and see, Elric. Look!"

Reluctantly, the albino moved to where Werther peered and pointed.

The entire landscape was filled with a monstrous battle. Creatures of all kinds and all combinations tore at one another with huge teeth and claws. Shapeless things slithered and hopped; giants, naked but for helmets and greaves, slashed at these beasts with great broadswords and axes, but were borne down. Flame and black smoke drifted everywhere. There was a smell. The stink of blood?

"What do you miss most?" asked the female. She pressed a soft body against him. He pretended not to be aware of it. He knew what magic flesh could hide on a she-witch.

"I miss peace," said Elric almost to himself, "and I miss war. For in battle I find a kind of peace . . ."

"Very good!" Bishop Castle applauded. "You are beginning to learn our ways. You will soon become one of our best conversationalists."

Elric touched the hilt of Stormbringer, hoping to feel it grow warm and vibrant under his hand, but it was still, impotent in the Realm of Chaos. He uttered a heavy sigh.

"You are an adventurer, then, in your own world?" said the Duke of Queens. He was bluff. He had changed his beard to an ordinary sort of black and was wearing a scarlet costume; quilted doublet and tight-fitting hose, with a blue and white ruff, an elaborately feathered hat on his head. "I, too, am something of a vagabond. As far, of course, as it is possible to be here. A buccaneer, of sorts. That is, my actions are in the main bolder than those of my fellows. More spectacular. Vulgar. Like yourself, sir. I admire your costume."

Elric knew that this Duke of Hell was referring to the fact that he affected the costume of the southern barbarian, that he did not wear the more restrained colours and more cleverly wrought silks and metals of his own folk. He gave tit for tat at this time. He bowed.

"Thank you, sir. Your own clothes rival mine."

"Do you think so?" The hell-lord pretended pleasure. If Elric had not known better, the creature would seem to be swelling with pride.

"Look!" cried Werther again. "Look, Lord Elric— we are attacked."

Elric whirled.

From below were rising oddly-wrought vessels— something like ships, but with huge round wheels at their sides, like the wheels of water-clocks he had seen once in Pikarayd. Coloured smoke issued from chimneys mounted on their decks which swarmed with huge birds dressed in human clothing. The birds had multi-coloured plumage, curved beaks, and they held swords in their claws, while on their heads were strangely shaped black hats on which were blazed skulls with crossed bones beneath.

"Heave to!" squawked the birds. "Or we'll put a shot across your bowels!"

"What can they be?" cried Bishop Castle.

"Parrots," said Werther de Goethe soberly. "Otherwise known as the hawks of the sea. And they mean us no good."

Mistress Christia blinked.

"Don't you mean pirates, dear?"

Elric took a firm grip on his sword. Some of the words the Chaos Lords used were absolutely meaningless to him. But whether the attacking creatures were of their own conception, or whether they were true enemies of his captors, Elric prepared to do bloody battle. His spirits improved. At least here was something substantial to fight.

7. In Which Mrs. Persson Becomes Anxious About the Future of the Universe

LORD JAGGED of Canaria was nowhere to be found. His huge castle, of gold and yellow spires, an embellished replica of Kings Cross station, was populated entirely by his quaint robots, whom Jagged found at once more mysterious and more trustworthy than android or human servants, for they could answer only according to a limited programme.

Una suspected that Jagged was, himself, upon some mission, for he, too, was a member of the League of Temporal Adventures. But she needed aid. Somehow she had to return Elric to his own dimensions without creating further disruptions in the fabric of Time and Space. The Conjunction was not due yet and, if things got any worse, might never come. So many plans depended on the Conjunction of the Million Spheres that she could not risk its failure. But she could not reveal too much either to Elric or his hosts. As a Guild member she was sworn to the utmost and indeed necessary secrecy. Even here at the End of Time there were certain laws which could be disobeyed only at enormous risk. Words alone were dangerous when they described ideas concerning the nature of Time.

She racked her brains. She considered seeking out Jherek Carnelian, but then remembered that he had scarcely begun to understand his own destiny. Besides, there were certain similarities between Jherek and Elric which she could only sense at present. It would be best to go cautiously there.

She decided that she had no choice. She must return to the Time Centre and see if they could detect Lord Jagged for her.

She brought the necessary co-ordinates together in her mind and concentrated. For a moment all memories, all sense of identity left her.

Sergeant Alvarez was beside himself. His screens were no longer completely without form. Instead, peculiar shapes could be seen in the arrangements of lines. Una thought she saw faces, beasts, landscapes. That had never occurred before. The instruments, at least, had remained sane, even as they recorded insanity.

"It's getting worse," said Alvarez. "You've hardly any Time left. What there is, I've managed to borrow for you. Did you contact the rogue?"

She nodded. "Yes. But getting him to return . . . I want you to find Jagged."

"Jagged? Are you sure?"

"It's our only chance, I think."

Alvarez sighed and bent a tense back over his controls.

8. In Which Elric and Werther Fight Side By Side Against Almost Overwhelming Odds

SOMEWHERE, IT seemed to Elric, as he parried and thrust at the attacking bird-monsters, rich and rousing music played. It must be a delusion, brought on by battle-madness. Blood and feathers covered the carriage. He saw the one called Christia carried off screaming. Bishop Castle had disappeared. Gaf had gone. Only the three of them, shoulder to shoulder, continued to fight. What was disconcerting to Elric was that Werther and the Duke of Queens bore swords absolutely identical to Stormbringer. Perhaps they were the legendary Brothers of the Black Sword, said to reside in Chaos?

He was forced to admit to himself that he experienced a sense of comradeship with these two, who were braver than most in defending themselves against such dreadful, unlikely monsters—perhaps some creation of their own which had turned against them.

Having captured the Lady Christia, the birds began to return to their own craft.

"We must rescue her!" cried Werther as the flying ships began to retreat. "Quickly! In pursuit!"

"Should we not seek reinforcements?" asked Elric, further impressed by the courage of this Chaos Lord.

"No time!" cried the Duke of Queens. "After them!"

Werther shouted to his vessel. "Follow those ships!" The vessel did not move.

"It has an enchantment on it," said Werther. "We are stranded! Ah, and I loved her so much!"

Elric became suspicious again. Werther had shown no signs, previously, of any affection for the female.

"You loved her?"

"From a distance," Werther explained. "Duke of Queens, what can we do? Those parrots will ransom her savagely and mishandle her objects of virtue!"

"Dastardly poltroons!" roared the huge duke.

Elric could make little sense of this exchange. It dawned on him, then, that he could still hear the rousing music. He looked below. On some sort of dais in the middle of the bizarre landscape a large group of musicians was assembled. They played on, apparently oblivious of what happened above. This was truly a world dominated by Chaos.

Their ship began slowly to fall towards the band. It lurched. Elric gasped and clung to the side as they struck yielding ground and bumped to a halt.

The Duke of Queens, apparently elated, was already scrambling overboard. "There! We can follow on those mounts."

Tethered near the dais was a herd of creatures bearing some slight resemblance to horses but in a variety of dazzling, metallic colours, with horns and bony ridges on their backs. Saddles and bridles of alien workmanship showed that they were domestic beasts, doubtless belonging to the musicians.

"They will want some payment from us, surely," said Elric, as they hurried towards the horses.

"Ah, true!" Werther reached into a purse at his belt and drew forth a handful of jewels. Casually he flung them towards the musicians and climbed into the saddle of the nearest beast. Elric and the Duke of Queens followed his example. Then Werther, with a whoop, was off in the direction in which the bird-monsters had gone.

The landscape of this world of Chaos changed rapidly as they rode. They galloped through forests of crystalline trees, over fields of glowing flowers, leapt rivers the colour of blood and the consistency of mercury, and their tireless mounts maintained a headlong pace which never faltered. Through clouds of boiling gas which wept, through rain, through snow, through intolerable heat, through shallow lakes in which oddly fashioned fish wriggled and gasped, until at last a range of mountains came in sight.

"There!" panted Werther, pointing with his own runesword. "Their lair. Oh, the fiends! How can we climb such smooth cliffs?"

It was true that the base of the cliffs rose some hundred feet before they became suddenly ragged, like the rotting teeth of the beggars of Nadsokor. They were of dusky, purple obsidian and so smooth as to reflect the faces of the three adventurers who stared at them in despair.

It was Elric who saw the steps cut into the side of the cliff.

"These will take us up some of the way, at least."

"It could be a trap," said the Duke of Queens. He, too, seemed to be relishing the opportunity to take action. Although a Lord of Chaos there was something about him that made Elric respond to a fellow spirit.

"Let them trap us," said Elric laconically. "We have our swords."

With a wild laugh, Werther de Goethe was the first to swing himself from his saddle and run towards the steps, leaping up them almost as if he had the power of flight. Elric and the Duke of Queens followed more slowly.

Their feet slipping in the narrow spaces not meant for mortals to climb, ever aware of the dizzying drop on their left, the three came at last to the top of the cliff and stood clinging to sharp crags, staring across a plain at a crazy castle rising into the clouds before them.

"Their stronghold," said Werther.

"What are these creatures?" Elric asked. "Why do they attack you? Why do they capture the Lady Christia?"

"They nurse an abiding hatred for us," explained the Duke of Queens, and looked expectantly at Werther, who added:

"This was their world before it became ours."

"And before it became theirs," said the Duke of Queens, "it was the world of the Yargtroon."

"The Yargtroon?" Elric frowned.

"They dispossessed the bodiless vampire goat-folk of Kia," explained Werther. "Who, in turn, destroyed—or thought they destroyed—the Grash-Tu-Xem, a race of Old Ones older than any Old Ones except the Elder Old Ones of Ancient Thriss."

"Older even than Chaos?" asked Elric.

"Oh, far older," said Werther.

"It's almost completely collapsed, it's so old," added the Duke of Queens.

Elric was baffled. "Thriss?"

"Chaos," said the duke.

Elric let a thin smile play about his lips. "You still mock me, my lord. The power of Chaos is the greatest there is, only equalled by the power of Law."

"Oh, certainly," agreed the Duke of Queens.

Elric became suspicious again. "Do you play with me, my lord?"

"Well, naturally, we try to please our guests . . ."

Werther interrupted. "Yonder doomy edifice holds the one I love. Somewhere within its walls she is incarcerated, while ghouls taunt at her and devils threaten."

"The bird-monsters . . .?" began Elric.

"Chimerae," said the Duke of Queens. "You saw only one of the shapes they assume."

Elric understood this. "Aha!"

"But how can we enter it?" Werther spoke almost to himself.

"We must wait until nightfall," said Elric, "and enter under the cover of darkness."

"Nightfall?" Werther brightened.

Suddenly they were in utter darkness.

Somewhere the Duke of Queens lost his footing and fell with a muffled curse.

9. In Which Mrs. Persson At Last Makes Contact With Her Old Friend

THEY STOOD together beneath the striped awning of the tent while a short distance away armoured men, mounted on armoured horses, jousted, were injured or died. The two members wore appropriate costumes for the period. Lord Jagged looked handsome in his surcoat and mail, but Una Persson merely looked uncomfortable in her wimple and kirtle.

"I can't leave just now," he was saying. "I am laying the foundations for a very important development."

"Which will come to nothing unless Elric is returned," she said.

A knight with a broken lance thundered past, covering them in dust.

"Well played Sir Holger!" called Lord Jagged. "An ancestor of mine, you know," he told her.

"You will not be able to recognise the world of the End of Time when you return, if this is allowed to continue," she said.

"It's always difficult, isn't it?" But he was listening to her now.

"These disruptions could as easily affect us and leave us stranded," she added. "We would lose any freedom we have gained."

He bit into a pomegranate and offered it to her. "You can only get these in this area. Did you know? Impossible to find in England. In the thirteenth century, at any rate. The idea of freedom is such a nebulous one, isn't it? Most of the time when angry people are speaking of 'freedom' what they are actually asking for is much simpler—respect. Do those in authority or those with power ever really respect those who do not have power?" He paused. "Or do they mean 'power' and not 'freedom.' Or are they the same . . .?"

"Really, Jagged, this is no time for self-indulgence."

He looked about him. "There's little else to do in the Middle East in the thirteenth century, I assure you, except eat pomegranates and philosophise . . ."

"You must come back to the End of Time."

He wiped his handsome chin. "Your urgency," he said, "worries me, Una. These matters should be handled with delicacy—slowly . . ."

"The entire fabric will collapse unless he is returned to his own dimension. He is an important factor in the whole plan."

"Well, yes, I understand that."

"He is, in one sense at least, your protégé."

"I know. But not my responsibility."

"You must help," she said.

There was a loud bang and a crash.

A splinter flew into Mrs. Persson's eye.

"Oh, zounds!" she said.

10. In Which The Castle Is Assaulted And The Plot Thickened

A MOON had appeared above the spires of the castle which seemed to Elric to have changed its shape since he had first seen it. He meant to ask his companions for an explanation, but at present they were all sworn to silence as they crept nearer. From within the castle burst light, emanating from guttering brands stuck into brackets on the walls. There was laughter, noise of feasting. Hidden behind a rock they peered through one large window and inspected the scene within.

The entire hall was full of men wearing identical costumes. They had black skull caps, loose white blouses and trousers, black shoes. Their eyebrows were black in dead white faces, even paler than Elric's and they had bright red lips.

"Aha," whispered Werther, "the parrots are celebrating their victory. Soon they will be too drunk to know what is happening to them."

"Parrots?" said Elric. "What is that word?"

"Pierrots, he means," said the Duke of Queens. "Don't you, Werther?" There were evidently certain words which did not translate easily into the High Speech of Melniboné.

"Sshh," said the Last Romantic, "they will capture us and torture us to death if they detect our presence."

They worked their way around the castle. It was guarded at intervals by gigantic warriors whom Elric at first mistook for statues, save that, when he looked closely, he could see them breathing very slowly. They were unarmed, but their fists and feet were disproportionately large and could crush any intruder they detected.

"They are sluggish, by the look of them," said Elric. "If we are quick, we can run beneath them and enter the castle before they realise it. Let me try first. If I succeed, you follow."

Werther clapped his new comrade on the back. "Very well."

Elric waited until the nearest guard halted and spread his huge feet apart, then he dashed forward, scuttling like an insect between the giant's legs and flinging himself through a dimly lit window. He found himself in some sort of storeroom. He had not been seen, though the guard cocked his ear for half a moment before resuming his pace.

Elric looked cautiously out and signalled to his companions. The Duke of Queens waited for the guard to stop again, then he, too, made for the window and joined Elric. He was panting and grinning. "This is wonderful," he said.

Elric admired his spirit. There was no doubt that the guard could crush any of them to a pulp, even if (as still nagged at his brain) this was all some sort of complicated illusion.

Another dash, and Werther was with them.

Cautiously, Elric opened the door of the storeroom. They looked onto a deserted landing. They crossed the landing and looked over a balustrade. They had expected to see another hall, but instead there was a miniature lake on which floated the most beautiful miniature ship, all mother-of-pearl, brass and ebony, with golden sails and silver masts. Surrounding this ship were mermaids and mermen bearing trays of exotic food (reminding Elric how hungry he still was) which they fed to the ship's only passenger, Mistress Christia.

"She is under an enchantment," said Elric. "They beguile her with illusions so that she will not wish to come with us even if we do rescue her. Do you know no counter-spells?"

Werther thought for a moment. Then he shook his head.

"You must be very minor Lords of Chaos," said Elric, biting his lower lip.

From the lake, Mistress Christia giggled and drew one of the mermaids towards her. "Come here, my pretty piscine!"

"Mistress Christia!" hissed Werther de Goethe.

"Oh!" The captive widened her eyes (which were now both large and blue). "At last!"

"You wish to be rescued?" said Elric.

"Rescued? Only by you, most alluring of albinoes!"

Elric hardened his features. "I am not the one who loves you, madam."

"What? I am loved? By whom? By you, Duke of Queens?"

"Sshh," said Elric. "The demons will hear us."

"Oh, of course," said Mistress Christia gravely, and fell silent for a second. "I'll get rid of all this, shall I?"

And she touched one of her rings.

Ship, lake and merfolk were gone. She lay on silken cushions, attended by monkeys.

"Sorcery!" said Elric. "If she has such power, then why—?"

"It is limited," explained Werther. "Merely to such tricks."

"Quite," said Mistress Christia.

Elric glared at them. "You surround me with illusions. You make me think I am aiding you, when really . . ."

"No, no!" cried Werther. "I assure you, Lord Elric, you have our greatest respect—well, mine at least—we are only attempting to—"

There was a roar from the gallery above. Rank upon rank of grinning demons looked down upon them. They were armed to the teeth.

"Hurry!" The Duke of Queens leapt to the cushions and seized Mistress Christia, flinging her over his shoulder. "We can never defeat so many!"

The demons were already rushing down the circular staircase. Elric, still not certain whether his new friends deceived him or not, made a decision. He called to the Duke of Queens. "Get her from the castle. We'll keep them from you for a few moments, at least." He could not help himself. He behaved impulsively.

The Duke of Queens, sword in one hand, Mistress Christia over the other shoulder, ran into a narrow passage. Elric and Werther stood together as the demons rushed down on them. Blade met blade. There was an unbearable shrilling of steel mingled with the cacklings and shrieks of the demons as they gnashed their teeth and rolled their eyes and slashed at the pair with swords, knives and axes. But worst of all was the smell. The dreadful smell of burning flesh which filled the air and threatened to choke Elric. It came from the demons. The smell of Hell. He did his best to cover his nostrils as he fought, certain that the smell must overwhelm him before the swords. Above him was a set of metal rungs fixed into the stones, leading high into a kind of a chimney. As a pause came he pointed upward to Werther, who understood him. For a moment they managed to drive the demons back. Werther jumped onto Elric's shoulders (again displaying a strange lightness) and reached down to haul the albino after him.

While the demons wailed and cackled below, they began to climb the chimney.

They climbed for nearly fifty feet before they found themselves in a small, round room whose windows looked out over the purple crags and, beyond them, to a scene of bleak rocky pavements pitted with holes, like some vast unlikely cheese.

And there, rolling over this relatively flat landscape, in full daylight (for the sun had risen) was the Duke of Queens in a carriage of brass and wood, studded with jewels, and drawn by two bovine creatures which looked to Elric as if they might be the fabulous oxen of mythology who had drawn the warchariot of his ancestors to do battle with the emerging nations of mankind.

Mistress Christia was beside the Duke of Queens. They seemed to be waiting for Elric and Werther.

"It's impossible," said the albino. "We could not get out of this tower, let alone those crags. I wonder how they managed to move so quickly and so far. And where did the chariot itself come from?"

"Stolen, no doubt, from the demons," said Werther.

"See, there are wings here." He indicated a heap of feathers in the corner of the room. "We can use those."

"What wizardry is this?" said Elric. "Man cannot fly on bird wings."

"With the appropriate spell he can," said Werther. "I am not that well versed in the magic arts, of course, but let me see . . ." He picked up one set of wings. They were soft and glinted with subtle, rainbow colours. He placed them on Elric's back, murmuring his spell:

Oh, for the wings, for the wings of a dove,
To carry me to the one I love . . .

"There!" He was very pleased with himself. Elric moved his shoulders and his wings began to flap. "Excellent! Off you go, Elric. I'll join you in a moment."

Elric hesitated, then saw the head of the first demon emerging from the hole in the floor. He jumped to the window ledge and leapt into space. The wings sustained him. Against all logic he flew smoothly towards the waiting chariot and behind him, came Werther de Goethe. At the windows of the tower the demons crowded, shaking fists and weapons as their prey escaped them.

Elric landed rather awkwardly beside the chariot and was helped aboard by the Duke of Queens. Werther joined them, dropping expertly amongst them. He removed the wings from the albino's back and nodded to the Duke of Queens who yelled at the oxen, cracking his whip as they began to move.

Mistress Christia flung her arms about Elric's neck. "What courage! What resourcefulness!" she breathed. "Without you, I should now be ruined!"

Elric sheathed Stormbringer. "We all three worked

together for your rescue, madam." Gently he removed her arms. Courteously he bowed and leaned against the far side of the chariot as it bumped and hurtled over the peculiar rocky surface.

"Swifter! Swifter!" called the Duke of Queens casting urgent looks backward. "We are followed!"

From the disappearing tower there now poured a host of flying, gibbering things. Once again the creatures had changed shape and had assumed the form of striped, winged cats, all glaring eyes, fangs and extended claws.

The rock became viscous, clogging the wheels of the chariot, as they reached what appeared to be a silvery road, flowing between the high trees of an alien forest already touched by a weird twilight.

The first of the flying cats caught up with them, slashing.

Elric drew Stormbringer and cut back. The beast roared in pain, blood streaming from its severed leg, its wings flapping in Elric's face as it hovered and attempted to snap at the sword.

The chariot rolled faster, through the forest to green fields touched by the moon. The days were short, it seemed, in this part of Chaos. A path stretched skyward. The Duke of Queens drove the chariot straight up it, heading for the moon itself.

The moon grew larger and larger and still the demons pursued them, but they could not fly as fast as the chariot which went so swiftly that sorcery must surely speed it. Now they could only be heard in the darkness behind and the silver moon was huge.

"There!" called Werther. "There is safety!"

On they raced until the moon was reached, the

oxen leaping in their traces, galloping over the gleaming surface to where a white palace awaited them.

"Sanctuary," said the Duke of Queens. And he laughed a wild, full laugh of sheer joy.

The palace was like ivory, carved and wrought by a million hands, every inch covered with delicate designs.

Elric wondered. "Where is this place?" he asked. "Does it lie outside the Realm of Chaos?"

Werther seemed non-plussed. "You mean our world?"

"Aye."

"It is still part of our world," said the Duke of Queens.

"Is the palace to your liking?" asked Werther.

"It is lovely."

"A trifle pale for my own taste," said the Last Romantic. "It was Mistress Christia's idea."

"You built this?" the albino turned to the woman. "When?"

"Just now." She seemed surprised.

Elric nodded. "Aha. It is within the power of Chaos to create whatever whims it pleases."

The chariot crossed a white drawbridge and entered a white courtyard. In it grew white flowers. They dismounted and entered a huge hall, white as bone, in which red lights glowed. Again Elric began to suspect mockery, but the faces of the Chaos lords showed only pleasure. He realised that he was dizzy with hunger and weariness, as he had been ever since he had been flung into this terrible world where no shape was constant, no idea permanent.

"Are you hungry?" asked Mistress Christia.

He nodded. And suddenly the room was filled by a long table on which all kinds of food were heaped—

and everything, meats and fruits and vegetables, was white.

Elric moved to take the seat she indicated and he put some of the food on a silver plate and he touched it to his lips and he tasted it. It was delicious. Forgetting suspicion, he began to eat heartily, trying not to consider the colourless quality of the meal. Werther and the Duke of Queens also took some food, but it seemed they ate only from politeness. Werther glanced up at the faraway roof. "What a wonderful tomb this would make," he said. "Your imagination improves, Mistress Christia."

"Is this your domain?" asked Elric. "The moon?"

"Oh, no," she said. "It was all made for the occasion."

"Occasion?"

"For your adventure," she said. Then she fell silent.

Elric became grave. "Those demons? They were not your enemies. They belong to you!"

"Belong?" said Mistress Christia. She shook her head.

Elric frowned and pushed back his plate. "I am, however, most certainly your captive." He stood up and paced the white floor. "Will you not return me to my own plane?"

"You would come back almost immediately," said Werther de Goethe. "It is called the Morphail Effect. And if you did not come here, you would yet remain in your own future. It is in the nature of Time."

"This is nonsense," said Elric. "I have left my own realm before and returned—though admittedly memory becomes weak, as with dreams poorly recalled."

"No man can go back in Time," said the Duke of Queens. "Ask Brannart Morphail."

"He, too, is a Lord of Chaos?"

"If you like. He is a colleague."

"Could he not return me to my realm? He sounds a clever being."

"He could not and he would not," said Mistress Christia. "Haven't you enjoyed your experiences here so far?"

"Enjoyed?" Elric was astonished. "Madam, I think . . . Well, what has happened this day is not what we mortals would call 'enjoyment'!"

"But you *seemed* to be enjoying yourself," said the Duke of Queens in some disappointment. "Didn't he, Werther?"

"You were much more cheerful through the whole episode," agreed the Last Romantic. "Particularly when you were fighting the demons."

"As with many time-travellers who suffer from anxieties," said Mistress Christia, "you appeared to relax when you had something immediate to capture your attention . . ."

Elric refused to listen. This was clever Chaos talk, meant to deceive him and take his mind from his chief concern.

"If I was any help to you," he began, "I am, of course . . ."

"He isn't very grateful," Mistress Christia pouted.

Elric felt madness creeping nearer again. He calmed himself.

"I thank you for the food, madam. Now, I would sleep."

"Sleep?" she was disconcerted. "Oh! Of course. Yes. A bedroom?"

"If you have such a thing."

"As many as you like." She moved a stone on one of her rings. The walls seemed to draw back to show bedchamber after bedchamber, in all manner of styles, with beds of every shape and fashion. Elric controlled his temper. He bowed, thanked her, said goodnight to the two lords and made for the nearest bed.

As he closed the door behind him, he thought he heard Werther de Goethe say: "We must try to think of a better entertainment for him when he wakes up."

11. In Which Mrs. Persson Witnesses The First Sign Of The Megaflow's Disintegration

IN CASTLE CANARIA Lord Jagged unrolled his antique charts. He had had them drawn for him by a baffled astrologer in 1590. They were one of his many affectations. At the moment, however, they were of considerably greater use than Alvarez's electronics.

While he used a wrist computer to check his figures, Una Persson looked out of the window of Castle Canaria and wondered who had invented this particular landscape. A green and orange sun cast sickening light over the herds of grazing beasts who resembled, from this distance at any rate, nothing so much as gigantic human hands. In the middle of the scene was raised some kind of building in the shape of a vast helmet, vaguely Greek in conception. Beyond that was a low, grey moon. She turned away.

"I must admit," said Lord Jagged, "that I had not understood the extent . . ."

"Exactly," she said.

"You must forgive me. A certain amount of amnesia—euphoria, perhaps?—always comes over one in these very remote periods."

"Quite."

He looked up from the charts. "We've a few hours at most."

Her smile was thin, her nod barely perceptible.

While she made the most of having told him so, Lord Jagged frowned, turned a power ring and produced an already lit pipe which he placed thoughtfully in his mouth, taking it out again almost immediately. "That wasn't Dunhill Standard Medium." He laid the pipe aside.

There came a loud buzzing noise from the window. The scene outside was disintegrating as if melting on glass. An eerie golden light spread everywhere, flooding from an apex of deeper gold, as if forming a funnel.

"That's a rupture," said Lord Jagged. His voice was tense. He put his arm about her shoulders. "I've never seen anything of the size before."

Rushing towards them along the funnel of light there came an entire city of turrets and towers and minarets in a wide variety of pastel colours. It was set into a saucer-shaped base which was almost certainly several miles in circumference.

For a moment the city seemed to retreat. The golden light faded. The city remained, some distance away, swaying a little as if on a gentle tide, a couple of thousand feet above the ground, the grey moon below it.

"That's what I call megaflow distortion," said Una Persson in that inappropriately facetious tone adopted by those who are deeply frightened.

"I recognise the period." Jagged drew a telescope from his robes. "Second Candlemaker's Empire, mainly based in Arcturus. This is a village by their standards. After all, Earth was merely a rural park during that time." He retreated into academe, his own response to fear.

Una craned her head. "Isn't that some sort of

vehicle heading towards the city. From the moon—good heavens, they've spotted it already. Are they going to try to put the whole thing into a menagerie?"

Jagged had the advantage of the telescope. "I think not." He handed her the instrument.

Through it she saw a scarlet and black chariot borne by what seemed to be some form of flying fairground horses. In the chariot, armed to the teeth with lances, bows, spears, swords, axes, morningstars, maces and almost every other barbaric hand-weapon, clad in quasi-mythological armour, were Werther de Goethe, the Duke of Queens and Elric of Melniboné.

"They're attacking it!" she said faintly. "What will happen when the two groups intersect?"

"Three groups," he pointed out. "Untangling that in a few hours is going to be even harder."

"And if we fail?"

He shrugged. "We might just as well give ourselves up to the biggest chronoquake the universe has ever experienced."

"You're exaggerating," she said.

"Why not? Everyone else is."

12. The Attack On The Citadel Of The Skies

"MELNIBONÉ! MELNIBONÉ"! cried the albino as the chariot circled over the spires and turrets of the city. They saw startled faces below. Strange engines were being dragged through the narrow streets.

"Surrender!" Elric demanded.

"I do not think they can understand us," said the Duke of Queens. "What a find, eh? A whole city from the past!"

Werther had been reluctant to embark on an adventure not of his own creation, but Elric, realising that here at last was a chance of escape, had been anxious to begin. The Duke of Queens had, in an instant, aided the albino by producing costumes, weapons, transport. Within minutes of the city's appearance, they had been on their way.

Exactly why Elric wished to attack the city, Werther could not make out, unless it was some test of the Melnibonéan's to see if his companions were true allies or merely pretending to have befriended him. Werther was learning a great deal from Elric, much more than he had ever learned from Mongrove, whose ideas of angst were only marginally less notional than Werther's own.

A broad, flat blue ray beamed from the city. It singed one wheel of the chariot.

"Ha! They make sorcerous weapons," said Elric. "Well, my friends. Let us see you counter with your own power."

Werther obediently imitated the blue ray and sent it back from his fingers, slicing the tops off several towers. The Duke of Queens typically let loose a different coloured ray from each of his extended ten fingers and bored a hole all the way through the bottom of the city so that fields could be seen below. He was pleased with the effect.

"This is the power of the Gods of Chaos!" cried Elric, a familiar elation filling him as the blood of old Melniboné was fired. "Surrender!"

"Why do you want them to surrender?" asked the Duke of Queens in some disappointment.

"Their city evidently has the power to fly through the dimensions. If I became its lord I can force it to return to my own plane," said Elric reasonably.

"The Morphail Effect . . ." began Werther, but

realised he was spoiling the spirit of the game. "Sorry."

The blue ray came again, but puttered out and faded before it reached them.

"Their power is gone!" cried Elric. "Your sorcery defeats them, my lords. Let us land and demand they honour us as their new rulers."

With a sigh, Werther ordered the chariot to set down in the largest square. Here they waited until a few of the citizens began to arrive, cautious and angry, but evidently in no mood to give any further resistance.

Elric addressed them. "It was necessary to attack and conquer you, for I must return to my own Realm, there to fulfill my great destiny. If you will take me to Melniboné, I will demand nothing further from you."

"One of us really ought to take a translation pill" said Werther. "These people probably have no idea where they are."

A meaningless babble came from the citizens. Elric frowned. "They understand not the High Speech," he said. "I will try the Common Tongue." He spoke in a language neither Werther, the Duke of Queens nor the citizens of this settlement could understand.

He began to show signs of frustration. He drew his sword Stormbringer. "By the Black Sword, know that I am Elric, last of the royal line of Melniboné! You must obey me. Is there none here who understands the High Speech?"

Then, from the crowd, stepped a being far taller than the others. He was dressed in robes of dark blue and deepest scarlet and his face was haughty, beautiful and full of evil.

"I speak the High Tongue," he said.

Werther and the Duke of Queens were non-plussed. This was no one they recognised.

Elric gestured. "You are the ruler of the city?"

"Call me that, if you will."

"Your name?"

"I am known by many names. And you know me, Elric of Melniboné, for I am your lord and your friend."

"Ah," said Elric lowering his sword, "this is the greatest deception of them all. I am a fool."

"Merely a mortal," said the newcomer, his voice soft, amused and full of a subtle arrogance. "Are these the renegades who helped you?"

"Renegades?" said Werther. "Who are you, sir?"

"You should know me, rogue lords. You aid a mortal and defy your brothers of Chaos."

"Eh?" said the Duke of Queens. "I haven't got a brother."

The stranger ignored him. "Demigods who thought that by helping this mortal they could threaten the power of the Greater Ones."

"So you did aid me against your own," said Elric. "Oh, my friends!"

"And they shall be punished!"

Werther began: "We regret any damage to your city. After all, you were not invited . . ."

The Duke of Queens was laughing. "Who are you? What disguise is this?"

"Know me for your master." The eyes of the stranger glowed with myriad fires. "Know me for Arioch, Duke of Hell!"

"Arioch!" Elric became filled with a strange joy. "Arioch! I called upon thee and was not answered!"

"I was not in this Realm," said the Duke of Hell.

"I was forced to be absent. And while I was gone, fools thought to displace me."

"I really cannot follow all this," said the Duke of Queens. He set aside his mace. "I must confess I become a trifle bored, sir. If you will excuse me."

"You will not escape me." Arioch lifted a languid hand and the Duke of Queens was frozen to the ground, unable to move anything save his eyes.

"You are interfering, sir, with a perfectly—" Werther too was struck dumb and paralysed.

But Elric refused to quail. "Lord Arioch, I have given you blood and souls. You owe me . . ."

"I owe you nothing, Elric of Melniboné. Nothing I do not choose to owe. You are my slave . . ."

"No," said Elric. "I serve you. There are old bonds. But you cannot control me, Lord Arioch, for I have a power within me which you fear. It is the power of my very mortality."

The Duke of Hell shrugged. "You will remain in the Realm of Chaos forever. Your mortality will avail you little here."

"You need me in my own Realm, to be your agent. That, too, I know, Lord Arioch."

The handsome head lowered a fraction as if Arioch considered this. The beautiful lips smiled. "Aye, Elric. It is true that I need you to do my work. For the moment it is impossible for the Lords of Chaos to interfere directly in the world of mortals, for we should threaten our own existence. The rate of entropy would increase beyond even our control. The day has not yet come when Law and Chaos must decide the issue once and for all. But it will come soon enough for you, Elric."

"And my sword will be at your service, Lord Arioch."

"Will it, Elric?"

Elric was surprised by this doubting tone. He had always served Chaos, as his ancestors had. "Why should I turn against you? Law has no attractions for one such as Elric of Melniboné."

The Duke of Hell was silent.

"And there is the bargain," added Elric. "Return me to my own Realm, Lord Arioch, so that I might keep it."

Arioch sighed. "I am reluctant."

"I demand it," bravely said the albino.

"Oho!" Arioch was amused. "Well, mortal, I'll reward your courage and I'll punish your insolence. The reward will be that you are returned from whence you came, before you called on Chaos in your battle with that pathetic wizard. The punishment is that you will recall every incident that occurred since then—but only in your dreams. You will be haunted by the puzzle for the rest of your life—and you will never for a moment be able to express what mystifies you."

Elric smiled. "I am already haunted by a curse of that kind, my lord."

"Be that as it may, I have made my decision."

"I accept it," said the albino, and he sheathed his sword, Stormbringer.

"Then come with me," said Arioch, Duke of Hell. And he drifted forward, took Elric by the arm, and lifted them both high into the sky, floating over distorted scenes, half-formed dream-worlds, the whims of the Lords of Chaos, until they came to a gigantic rock shaped like a skull. And through one of the eye-sockets Lord Arioch bore Elric of Melniboné. And down strange corridors that whispered and displayed all manner of treasures. And up into a landscape, a desert in which grew many strange plants, while overhead could be seen a land of snow and mountains, equally alien. And from his robes Arioch, Duke of Hell produced a wand and he bade Elric to take hold of the wand, which was hot to the touch and glittered, and he placed his own slender hand at the other end, and he murmured words which Elric could not understand and together they began to fade from the landscape, into the darkness of limbo where many eyes accused them, to an island in a grey and storm-tossed sea; an island littered with destruction and with the dead.

Then Arioch, Duke of Hell, laughed a little and vanished, leaving the Prince of Melniboné sprawled amongst corpses and ruins while heavy rain beat down upon him.

And in the scabbard at Elric's side, Stormbringer stirred and murmured once more.

13. In Which There Is A Small Celebration At The End Of Time

WERTHER DE GOETHE and the Duke of Queens blinked their eyes and found that they could move their heads. They stood in a large, pleasant room full of charts and ancient instruments. Mistress Christia was there, too.

Una Persson was smiling as she watched golden light fade from the sky. The city had disappeared, hardly any the worse for its experience. She had managed to save the two friends without a great deal of fuss, for the citizens had still been bewildered by what had happened to them. Because of the megaflow distortion, the Morphail Effect would not manifest itself. They would never understand where they had been or what had actually happened.

"Who on earth was that fellow who turned up?" asked the Duke of Queens. "Some friend of yours, Mrs. Persson? He's certainly no sportsman."

"Oh, I wouldn't agree. You could call him the ultimate sportsman," she said. "I am acquainted with him, as a matter of fact."

"It's not Jagged in disguise is it?" said Mistress Christia who did not really know what had gone on. "This is Jagged's castle—but where is Jagged?"

"You are aware how mysterious he is," Una answered. "I happened to be here when I saw that Werther and the Duke were in trouble in the city and was able to be of help."

Werther scowled (a very good copy of Elric's own scowl). "Well, it isn't good enough."

"It was a jolly adventure while it lasted, you must admit," said the Duke of Queens.

"It wasn't meant to be jolly," said Werther. "It was meant to be significant."

Lord Jagged entered the room. He wore his familiar yellow robes. "How pleasant," he said. "When did all of you arrive?"

"I have been here for some time," Mrs. Persson explained, "but Werther and the Duke of Queens . . ."

"Just got here," explained the duke. "I hope we're not intruding. Only we had a slight mishap and Mrs. Persson was good enough . . ."

"Always delighted," said the insincere lord. "Would you care to see my new—?"

"I'm on my way home," said the Duke of Queens. "I just stopped by. Mrs. Persson will explain."

"I, too," said Werther suspiciously, "am on my way back."

"Very well. Goodbye."

Werther summoned an aircar, a restrained figure of death, in rags with a sickle, who picked the three up in his hand and bore them towards a bleak horizon.

It was only days later, when he went to visit Mongrove to tell him of his adventures and solicit his friend's advice, that Werther realised he was still speaking High Melnibonéan. Some nagging thought remained with him for a long while after that. It concerned Lord Jagged, but he could not quite work out what was involved.

After this incident there were no further disruptions at the End of Time until the beginning of the story concerning Jherek Carnelian and Miss Amelia Underwood.

14. In Which Elric of Melniboné Recovers From a Variety of Enchantments and Becomes Determined to Return to the Dreaming City

ELRIC WAS awakened by the rain on his face. Wearily he peered around him. To left and right there were only the dismembered corpses of the dead, the Krettii and the Filkharian sailors destroyed during his battle with the halfbrute who had somehow gained so much sorcerous power. He shook his milk-white hair and he raised crimson eyes to the grey, boiling sky.

It seemed that Arioch had aided him, after all. The sorcerer was destroyed and he, Elric, remained alive. He recalled the sweet, bantering tones of his patron demon. Familiar tones, yet he could not remember what the words had been.

He dragged himself over the dead and waded

through the shallows towards the Filkharian ship
which still had some of its crew. They were, by now,
anxious to head out into open sea again rather than
face any more terrors on Sorcerer's Isle.

He was determined to see Cymoril, whom he loved,
to regain his throne from Yyrkoon, his cousin . . .

15. In Which A Brief Reunion Takes Place At the Time Centre

WITH THE manuscript of Colonel Pyat's rather dangerous volume of memoirs safely back in her brief-
case, Una Persson decided it was the right moment
to check into the Time Centre. Alvarez should be on
duty again and his instruments should be registering
any minor imbalances resulting from the episode
concerning the gloomy albino.

Alvarez was not alone. Lord Jagged was there, in
a disreputable Norfolk jacket and smoking a battered
briar. He had evidently been holidaying in Victorian
England. He was pleased to see her.

Alvarez ran his gear through all functions. "Sweet
and neat," he said. "It hasn't been as good since
I don't know when. We've you to thank for that,
Mrs. P.".

She was modest.

"Certainly not. Jagged was the one. Your disguise
was wonderful, Jagged. How did you manage to
imitate that character so thoroughly? It convinced
Elric. He really thought you were whatever it was—a
Chaos Duke?"

Jagged waved a modest hand.

"I mean," said Una, "it's almost as if you *were* this
fellow 'Arioch' . . ."

But Lord Jagged only puffed on his pipe and smiled
a secret and superior smile.

The Last Enchantment

THROUGH THE blue and hazy night ran a shuddering man. He clutched terror to him, his bloated eyes full of blood. First behind him and then seemingly ahead of him came the hungry chuckles, the high whispered words.

"Here toothsome. Here sweetmeat."

He swerved in another direction, moaning. Like a huge husk he was, like a hollow ornament of thin bone, with his great, rolling head swaying on his shoulders resembling a captive balloon, the wet cavern of his wide mouth fully open and gasping, the yellow spikes of teeth clashing in his head.

Awkwardly he ran, sometimes scuttling like a wounded spider, something lurching, mooing to himself through the tall and ancient forest, his feet sinking into the carpet of wet, pungent bracken and rotting roots. He held in his hand, that long, white, metal-coloured claw, a glowing black talisman, held it out and cried:

"Oh Teshwan—aid me, Teshwan. Aid me . . ."

In the sluggish brew that was the contents of his rolling skull a few words swam to the surface and seemed to lie there, moving with the tide of his mind. And the voice which spoke them was sardonic: *"How can Teshwan aid thee, little mortal?"*

But this relic of disoriented flesh could not form a coherent thought; could not answer save to scream its fear. So Teshwan took his presence away and it was left to the horseman to find the horror-crazed man.

Elric of Melniboné heard the voice and recognized the name. He sensed other, more ominous, denizens lurking about him in the forest.

Moodily he curled his hands about the reins of his mount and jerked its head, guiding it in the direction of the screams. He only casually considered aiding the man and he rode his horse toward him more from curiosity than anything. Elric was untroubled by the terrors that the forest held, regarding them as another, more normal man might regard the omnipresent song of birds and the rustle of small rodents in the undergrowth.

Great tremblings shuddered through Slorg's ruined body and he still heard the sharp whisperings. Were they carried on the air or were they slithering about in his jellied brain?

He gasped as he turned and saw the white-faced horseman riding like a grim, handsome god into the moon-glazed glade.

The horseman's long, sharply delineated skull was leperwhite, as if stripped of flesh, and his slightly slanting eyes gleamed crimson. He wore a jerkin of black velvet caught at the throat by a thin silver chain. His britches, too, were of black cloth, and his leather boots were high and shining. Over his shoulders was a high-collared cape of scarlet and a heavy longsword slapped at his side as he pulled his steed to a standstill. His long, flowing hair was as white as his face. The horseman was an albino.

The shock of confronting this new and more tangible figure jerked Slorg back into half-sanity and broken words sidled from his lips.

"Who are you? Aid me! I beg you, aid me!"

Elric laughed lightly. "Now why should I, my friend? Tell me that."

"I have been—been profaned—I am Slorg. I was once a man—but those . . ." He rocked his body and flung his rolling head backwards, the curved lids falling down to cover his bulging eyes. "I have been profaned . . ."

Elric leaned forward on the pommel of his saddle and said lazily: "This is none of my business, Master Slorg."

The great head darted forward, the eyes snapped open and Slorg's long lips writhed over his teeth like a camel's. "Address not me by a mundane title! I am Siletah Slorg—Siletah of Oberlorn—rightfully—rightfully."

The title was unknown to Elric.

"My apologies, O Siletah," he mocked, "for now I observe a man of rank."

"A man no longer," whispered Slorg and began to sob. "Help me."

"Are you, then, in danger?"

"Aye, danger—my kinsmen have set the Hungry Whisperers upon me, do you not hear them?"

And Elric cocked his head to listen. Yes, he heard sibilant voices now. *"Where are you, morsel?"*

"Oh, help me, help me," begged Slorg and lurched

toward Elric. The albino drew himself up and pulled his horse back.

"No closer," he warned. "I am Elric of Melniboné."

Slorg's tattered face squeezed itself into a frown. "Ah, the name and the face," he mumbled to himself, "the face and the name. Elric of Melniboné. *Outcast!*"

"Indeed," smiled Elric, "but no more than you, it seems. Now I must bid you farewell and suggest, by way of friendly advice, that you compose yourself soon. It is better to die with dignity, Siletah Slorg."

"I have powers, outcast of Melniboné—I have powers, still! Help me and I will tell you secrets—such secrets!"

Elric waved a disdainful hand. A moonbeam caught for an instant the flash of the rare actorios ring which reposed on his finger. "If you know me, you should also know that I'm no merchant to bargain. I ask nothing and give nothing. Farewell!"

"I warn you, Elric—I have one power left. I can send you screaming from this place—into another. It is the power which Teshwan gives all his servants—it is the one he never takes back!"

"Why not send your hungry friends into this other place?"

"They are not human. But if you leave me, I shall lay my last enchantment upon you."

Elric sighed. "Your last, perhaps, but not the last or the first to be laid upon me. Now I must go and searh for a quieter place than this where I can sleep undisturbed."

He turned his horse and his back on the shaking remnant of a man and rode away.

He heard Slorg calling again as he entered another

part of the forest, untainted by the Siletah or those
he had termed the Hungry Whisperers.

"Teshwan—return! Return to do me one last
service—a deed of vengeance—a part of our bargain,
Teshwan!"

A short time later Elric heard a thin, wailing scream
come flowing out of the night behind him and then
the whole forest seemed alive with horrible laughter.
Satiated, triumphant, chuckling.

His mood altered by his encounter, Elric rode through
night, not caring to sleep, and came out of the forest
in the morning, glad of the sight of the green plateau stretching ahead of him.

"Well," he mused, "Teshwan disdained to aid
Slorg and it seems there is no enchantment on me. I
am half regretful. Now Slorg resides in the bellies of
those he feared and his soul's at home in Hell."

Then the plateau changed quite suddenly to grey
rock.

Swiftly Elric wheeled his horse. The plateau and
the forest was behind him. He spurred his mount
quickly forward and the plateau and forest faded
away to leave a vast and lonely expanse of flat, grey
stone. Above him the sun had disappeared and the
sky was bright and white and cold.

"Now," said Elric grimly into silence, "it seems I
was wrong in my assumption."

The plateau—its atmosphere—reminded him of another environment in which he had once found himself. Then he remembered clearly a time years before
when he and two companions had sought an ancient volume called the Dead God's Book. Their questing had led them to a cavern guarded at its entrance

by the symbol of the Lords of Chaos. In that cavern they had discovered an underground sea which had had unnatural qualities. There was the same sense of a sardonically amused *presence* here as there had been in the Caverns of Chaos.

Teshwan was a Lord of Chaos.

Hastily Elric pulled his runesword Stormbringer from its thick scabbard.

The sword was dead.

Normally the blade, forged by unhuman smiths for Elric's royal ancestors, was alive with sentience—throbbing with the life force it had stolen from a hundred men and women whom Elric had slain. Once before it had been like this—in the Caverns of Chaos long ago.

Elric tightened his lips, then shrugged as he replaced the sword in its scabbard.

"In a world completely dominated by the Forces of Chaos," he said, "I cannot rely on the powers which normally aid me in my sorcery. Thank Arioch I have a good supply of drugs about me, or I would indeed be doomed."

In earlier times Elric had relied on his soul-stealing runesword to give him the energy which, as an albino, he lacked intrinsically, but recently he had rediscovered a cleaner way of counteracting his deficiency, by taking herbs he had discovered in the Forest of Troos where many unlikely things grew, both flora and fauna.

"By my father's plague-infested bones," he swore. "I must find a way off this granite plain and discover who, if anyone, rules in this world. I have heard of the powers invested in Teshwan's worshippers—and I seem to remember a hint of why the Lords of Chaos confer such peculiar talents upon them."

He shuddered.

He began to sing a ululating hate-song of old Melniboné. Elric's ancestors had been clever haters. And on he rode beneath the sunless sky.

He could not tell how much time had passed before he saw the figure standing out strongly against the featureless horizon.

Now on the flat waste of stone there were two points at which the monotony was broken.

Elric—white, black and scarlet on a grey gelding.

The morose man, black hair lying like a coat of lacquer on his rounded skull, dressed in green, a silver sword dangling in his right hand.

Elric approached the man who raised his eyes to regard the albino.

"This is a lonely place," said the stranger, sucking at his fleshy cheeks, and he stared at the ground again.

"True," replied Elric halting his horse. "Is this your world or were you sent here, also?"

"Oh, it's my world," said the man, without looking up. "Where are you bound?"

"For nowhere, seeking something. Where do you journey?"

"I—oh, I go to Kaneloon for the Rites, of course."

"All things, it is said, are possible in the World of Chaos," Elric murmured, "and yet this place seems unusually barren."

The man looked up suddenly, and jerking his lips into a smile, laughed sharply.

"The Rites will alter that, stranger. Did you not know that this is the Time of The Change, when the Lords of Chaos rest before re-forming the world into a fresh variety of patterns?"

"I did not know that," said Elric. "I have come here only recently."

"You wish to stay?"

"No."

"The Lords of Chaos are fickle. If you wished to stay they might not let you. Now that you are resolved to leave, they might keep you here. Farewell. You will find me therein!" He lifted his sword and pointed. A great palace of greenstone appeared at once. The man vanished.

"This, at least, will save me from boredom," Elric said philosophically, and rode towards the palace.

The many-pinnacled building towered above him, its highest points hazy and seeming to possess many forms, shifting as if blown by a wind. At the great arch of the entrance a huge giant, semi-transparent, with a red, scintillating skin, blocked his way. Over the archway, as if hanging in the air above the giant's proud head, was the Symbol of Chaos, a circle which produced many arrows pointing in all directions.

"Who visits the Palace of Kaneloon at the Time of the Change?" enquired the giant in a voice like limbo's music.

"Your masters, I gather, know me—for they aided their servant Slorg in sending me hither. But tell them it is Elric of Melniboné, nonetheless—Elric, destroyer of dreaming Imrryr, kinslayer and outcast. They will know me."

The giant appeared to shrink, to solidify and then to drift in a red mist, pouring like sentient smoke away from the portal and into the palace. And where he had been a portcullis manifested itself to guard the palace in the giant's absence.

Elric waited patiently until at length the portcullis vanished and the giant reformed himself.

"My masters order me to inform you that you may enter but that, having once come to the Palace of Kaneloon, you may never leave save under certain conditions."

"Those conditions?"

"Of these they will tell you if you enter. Are you reckless—or will you stand pondering?"

"I'll avail myself of their generosity," smiled Elric and spurred his nervous horse forward.

As he entered the courtyard, it appeared that the area within the palace was greater than that outside it. Not troubling to seek any mundane explanation for this phenomenon in a world dominated by the Lords of Chaos, Elric instead dismounted from his horse and walked for nearly a quarter of a mile until he reached the entrance of the main building. He climbed the steps swiftly and found himself in a vast hall which had walls of shifting flame.

In the glow from the fiery walls, there sat at a table at the far end of the hall nine men—or at least, men or not, they had assumed the form of men. Different in facial characteristics, they all had the same sardonic air. In the centre of these nine was the one who had first addressed Elric. He leaned forward and spoke words carefully from his red lips.

"Greetings to you, mortal," he said. "You are the first for some time to sit with the Lords of Chaos at the Time of the Change. Behold—there are others who have had the privilege."

A rent appeared in the wall of flame to disclose some thirty frozen human figures, some men and some women. They were petrified in positions of many kinds, but all had madness and terror in their eyes—and they were still alive, Elric knew.

He lifted his head.

"I would not be so impertinent, my lords, as to set myself beside you all insofar as powers are concerned, but you know that I am Elric of Melniboné and that my race is old; my deficient blood is the royal blood of the Kings of the Dreaming City. I have little pity or sentiment of any kind within me, for sentiment, whether love or hate, has served me badly in the past. I do not know what you require of me, and I thank you for your hospitality nonetheless, but I believe that I can conduct myself better in most ways than can any other mortal."

"Let us hope so, Elric of Melniboné, for we would not wish you to fail, know that. Besides, you are not fully mortal as humans understand the word. Now, know you that I be Teshwan, and these need not be named and may be addressed singly or collectively by the name of Lords of Chaos."

Elric bowed politely. "Lord Teshwan—my Lords of Chaos."

They returned his bow by slightly inclining their heads and broadening a trifle their sardonic, crooked smiles.

"Come," said Teshwan briskly, "sit here beside me and I will inform you of what we expect. You are more favoured than others have been, Elric, and, in truth, I welcomed the opportunity given me by my vengeful servant Slorg before he died."

Elric climbed upon the dais and seated himself in the chair which appeared beside Teshwan. About him the walls of flame soared and tumbled, mumbled and roared. Sometimes shadow engulfed them, sometimes they were bathed in light. For a while they all sat in silence, pondering.

At last Teshwan spoke.

"Now," he said decisively. "Here's the situation

in which we have decided to place you. You may leave only if you can create something which it has never occurred to us to create."

"But you, surely, are the Masters of Creation?" said Elric in puzzlement. "How may I do this?"

"Your first statement is not strictly true and in qualifying it I can give you a hint of the answer to your question. We of Chaos cannot make anything new—we may only experiment with combinations of that already created. Do you understand?"

"I do," said Elric.

"Only the Greatest Power, of which we know little more than do humans, can create fresh conceptions. The Greatest Power holds both Law and Chaos in perpetual balance, making us war only so that the scale will not be tilted too far to one side. We wish not for power—only for variety. Thus every time we weary of our domain and let our old creations fade and conceive new ones. If you can bring a fresh element to our domain, we shall free you. We create jokes and paradoxes. Conceive a better joke and a better paradox for our entertainment and you may leave here."

"Surely you expect the impossible from me?"

"You alone may assess the truth of your question. Now, we begin."

And Elric sat and watched, pondering his problem, as the great Lords of Chaos began their mighty experiments.

The walls of fire slowly flickered and faded and again he saw the vast and barren plain of flat stone. Then the air darkened and a sighing wind began to moan over the plain. In the sky clouds blossomed in myriad shapes, alien, dark, unfamiliar, blacks and smoky orange, at the same time familiar . . .

The rock heaved like lava, became liquid, rearing upwards and as it reared it became giants, mountains, ancient beasts, monsters, gryphons, basilisks, chimerae, unicorns. Forests bloomed, their growths huge and exotic, elephants flew and great birds crushed boiling mountains beneath their feet. Fingers of brilliant colour climbed the sky, criss-crossing and blending. A flight of wildly singing lions fell from the firmament towards the forest and soared upwards again, their music lonely.

As the forest melted to become an ocean, a vast army of wizened homunculae came tramping from its depths dragging boats behind them. For a short while they marched over the seething waters and then, with precision, began, in ordered style, to climb into the flaring sky. When they had all left the ocean behind them, they righted their boats, set their sails, laughed and screamed and shouted, waved their arms, climbed into the boats and with fantastic speed streamed towards the horizon.

All creation tumbled and poured, malleable in the Domain of Chaos. All was gusto, craze and roaring terror, love, hate and music mingled.

The sky shook with multi-coloured mirth, blossoming white shot through with veins of blue and purple and black, searing red, splattered with spreading flowers of yellow, smeared, smeared, smeared with ghoulish green. Across this seething backdrop sped bizarre shapes.

The Lords of Chaos shouted and sang their weird creation and Elric, shouting also, thought the frozen statues he had seen were weeping and laughing.

A grotesque combination of man and tree sent

roots streaming towards the earth to tug mountains from the caverns it exposed and set them, peak first, like inverted pyramids, into the ground. Upon the flat surfaces dancers appeared in bright rags which fluttered and flared around them. They were warped, unhuman, pale as dead beauty, grinning fixedly and then Elric saw the strings attached to their limbs and the silently laughing puppet-master bearlike and gigantic, controlling them. From another direction sped a small, blind figure bearing a scythe that was a hundred times bigger than the bearer. With a sweep, he cut the strings and, with that action, the whole faded to be replaced by a gushing brilliance of green and orange flame which formed itself into streamers of zigzagging disorder.

All this went on around them. The Lords of Chaos smiled to themselves now, as they created, but Elric frowned, watched with wonder and no little pleasure, but puzzled how he might emulate such feats.

For long hours the pageant of Chaos continued as the Lords took the elements of Elric's world and shook them about, turned them inside out, stood them on end, made startling, strange, beautiful, unholy combinations until they were satisfied with the constant movement of the scene about them, the perpetual shifting and changing. They had set a pattern that was no pattern, which would last until they became bored with their domain again and brought about another Time of the Change.

Then their heads turned and all regarded Elric expectantly.

Teshwan said a trifle wearily. "There—you have seen what we can do."

"You are artists, indeed," said Elric, "and I am so

amazed by what I have witnessed that I need a little time to think. Will you grant it me?"

"A little time—a little time only—we want to see what you prepare for us while the excitement is still upon us."

And Elric placed his white albino's head upon his fist and thought deeply.

Many ideas occurred to him, only to be discarded, but at length he straightened his back and said: "Give me the power to create and I will create."

So Teshwan said smilingly. "You have the power— use it well. A joke and a paradox is all we require."

"The reward for failure?"

"To be forever conscious."

At this, Elric shivered and put his mind to concentrating, searching his memory until a manlike figure formed before him. Then he placed features on its head and clothes on its body until there stood before Elric and the Lords of Chaos a perfect replica—of Elric.

Puzzledly, Teshwan said: "This is splendid impertinence, I grant you—but this is nothing new—you already sit there beside us."

"Indeed," replied Elric, "but look in the man's mind."

They frowned and did as he asked. Then, smiling, they nodded. "The paradox is good," said Teshwan, "and we see your point. We have, for an eternity, created the effect. You, in your pride and innocence, have created the cause. In that man's mind was all that could ever exist."

"You have noted the paradox?" asked Elric, anxious that the correct interpretation had been divulged.

"Of course. For though the mind contains the variety beloved of we of Chaos, it contains the order that those barren Lords of Law would foist on the world. Truly, young mortal, you have created everything with a stroke. And thank you, also, for the joke."

"The joke?"

"Why truly— the best joke is but a simple statement of truth. Farewell. Remember, friend mortal, that the Lords of Chaos are grateful to you."

And with that, the whole domain faded away and Elric stood on the grassy plain. In the distance he observed the city of Bakshaan which had been his original destination, and nearby was his horse to take him there.

He mounted, flapped the reins, and, as the grey gelding broke into a trot, he said to himself: "A joke indeed, but it is a pity that men do not laugh at it more often."

Reluctantly, he headed for the city.

The Secret Life of Elric of Melniboné

SOME YEARS ago, when I was about eighteen, I wrote a novel called *The Golden Barge*. This was an allegorical fantasy about a little man completely without self-knowledge and with little of any other kind, going down a seemingly endless river, following a great Golden Barge which he felt, if he caught it would contain all truth, all secrets, all solutions to his problems. On the journey he met various groups of people, had a love affair, and so on. Yet every action he took in order to reach the Golden Barge seemed to keep him farther away from it. The river represented Time, the barge was what mankind is always seeking outside itself (when it can be found inside itself), etc., etc. The novel had a sad ending, as such novels do. Also, as was clear when I'd finished it, my handling of many of the scenes was clumsy and immature. So I scrapped it and decided that in future my allegories would be intrinsic within a conventional narrative—that the best symbols were the symbols found in familiar objects. Like swords for instance.

Up until I was twenty or so, I had a keen interest in fantasy fiction, particularly Sword-and-Sorcery stories of the kind written by Robert E. Howard, Clark Ashton Smith and the like, but this interest began to wane as I became more interested in less directly sensational forms of literature, just as earlier my interest in Edgar Rice Burroughs' tales had waned. I could still enjoy one or two Sword-and-Sorcery tales, particularly Poul Anderson's *The Broken Sword* and Fritz Leiber's *Grey Mouser* stories. A bit before this casting off of old loyalties, I had been in touch with Sprague De Camp and Hans Santessen of *Fantastic Universe* about doing a new series of Conan tales.

I think it was in the autumn of 1960, when I was working for *Sexton Blake Library* and reading SF for *Suspense* (the short-lived companion to *Argosy*) that I bumped into a colleague at Fleetway Publications, Andy Vincent, who was an old friend of Harry Harrison's (who had also freelanced for Fleetway for some time). Andy told me he was meeting Harry and Ted Carnell in the Fleetway foyer and suggested I went along. As I remember, that was where I first met Harry. Previously, I'd sold a couple of stories to Ted, one in collaboration with Barry Bayley, and had had more bounced than bought. Later on in a pub, Ted and I were talking about Robert E. Howard and Ted said he'd been thinking of running some Conan-type stuff in *Science Fantasy*. I told him of the *Fantastic Universe* idea which had fallen through when *Fantastic Universe* folded, and said I still had the stuff I'd done and would he like to see it. He said he would. A couple of days later I sent him the first chapter and outline of a Conan story. To tell you the truth, writing in Howard's style had its limitations, as did his hero as far as I was concerned, and I wasn't looking forward to producing another 10,000 words of the story if Ted liked it.

Ted liked it—or at least he liked the writing, but there had been a misunderstanding. He hadn't wanted Conan—he had wanted something on the same lines.

This suited me much better. I decided that I would think up a hero as different as possible from the usual run of S-and-S heroes, and use the narrative as a vehicle for my own "serious' ideas. Many of these ideas, I realise now, were somewhat romantic and coloured by a long drawn-out and, to me, at the time, tragic love affair which hadn't quite finished its course and which was confusing and darkening my outlook. I was writing floods of hack work for Fleetway and was getting sometimes £70 or £80 a week which was going on drink mainly, and, as I remember, involved rather a lot of broken glass of one description or another. I do remember, with great pride, my main achievement of the winter of 1960 or 1961, which was to smash entirely an unbreakable plate-glass door in a well-known restaurant near Piccadilly. And the management apologised . . .

I mention this, to give a picture of my mood at the time of Elric's creaton. If you've read the early Elric stories in particular, you'll see that Elric's outlook was rather similar to mine. My point is, that Elric *was* me (the me of 1960–1, anyway) and the mingled qualities of betrayer and betrayed, the bewilderment about life in general, the search for some solution to it all, the expression of this bewilderment in terms of violence, cynicism and the need for revenge, were all characteristic of mine. So when I got the chance to write *The Dreaming City*, I was identifying very closely with my hero-villain. I thought myself something of an outcast (another romantic notion largely unsubstantiated now that I look back) and emphasised Elric's physical differences accordingly:

His bizarre dress was tasteless and gaudy, and did not match his sensitive face and long-fingered, almost delicate hands, yet he flaunted it since it emphasised that he did not belong in any company—that he was an outsider and an outcast. But, in reality, he had little need to wear such outlandish gear—for . . . (he) was a pure albino who drew his power from a secret and terrible source.

(Stealer of Souls, page 13)

The story was packed with personal symbols (as are all the stories bar a couple). The "secret and terrible source" was the sword *Stormbringer*, which symbolised my own and others tendency to rely on mental and physical crutches rather than cure the weakness at source. To go further, Elric, for me, symbolised the ambivalence of mankind in general, with its love-hates, its mean-generosity, its confident-bewilderment act. Elric is a thief who believes *himself* robbed, a lover who hates love. In short, he cannot be sure of the truth of anything, not even of his own emotions or ambitions. This is made much clearer in a story containing even more direct allegory, the second in the series, *While the Gods Laugh*. Unfortunately, Ted left out the verse from which the title was taken:

I, while the gods laugh, the world's vortex am;
Maelstrom of passions in that hidden sea,
Whose waves of all-time lap the coasts of me,
And in small compass the dark waters cram.

Mervyn Peake *(Shapes and Sounds)*

This, I think, gave more meaning to both title and story which involved a long quest after the Dead

God's Book—a mythical work alleged to contain all the knowledge of the universe, in which Elric feels, he will at last find the true meaning of life. He expresses this need in a somewhat rhetorical way. When the wingless woman Shaarilla asks him why he wants the book he replies:

"I desire, if you like, to know one of (misprinted as *or* in magazine version) two things. Does an ultimate God exist or not? Does Law or Chaos govern our lives? Man needs a God, so the philosophers tell us. Have they made one— or did one make them?" etc., etc.

Here, as in other passages, the bewilderment is expressed in metaphysical terms, for at that time, due mainly to my education I was very involved with mysticism. Also, the metaphysical terms suited the description of a Sword-and-Sorcery hero and his magical, low-technology world.

It may seem odd that I use such phrases as "at that time" and so on, as if I'm referring to the remote past, but in many ways, being a trifle more mature, perhaps, happily married with a better sense of direction, etc., all this *does* seem to have taken place in the remote past.

The Dead God's Book is eventually located in a vast underground world which I had intended as a womb-symbol, and after a philosophical conversation with the book's keeper, Elric discovers it. This passage is, to me now, rather overwritten, but, for better or worse:

It was a huge book—the Dead God's Book, its covers encrusted with alien gems from which the light sprang. It gleamed, it *throbbed* with light and brilliant colour.

"At last," Elric breathed. "At last—the truth!"

He stumbled forward like a man made stupid with drink, his pale hands reaching for the thing he sought with such savage bitterness. His hands touched the pulsating cover of the Book and, trembling, turned it back . . . With a crash, the cover fell to the floor, sending the bright gems skipping and dancing over the paving stone. *Beneath Elric's . . . hands lay nothing but a pile of yellowish dust.*

The Dead God's Book and the Golden Barge are one and the same. They have no real existence, save in the wishful imagination of mankind. There is, the story says, no Holy Grail which will transform a man overnight from bewildered ignorance to complete knowledge—the answer already is within him, if he cares to train himself to find it. A rather over-emphasised fact, throughout history, but one generally ignored all the same.

The Stealer of Souls, the third story, continues this theme, but brought in rather different kinds of symbols. Coupled with the Jungian symbols already inherent in any tale using direct mythic material, I used Freudian symbols, too. This was a cynical attempt and a rather vulgar attempt to make the series popular. It appeared to work. *The Stealer of Souls*, whatever else it may be, is one of the most pornographic stories I have ever written. In Freudian terms it is the description of, if you like, a night's lovemaking.

Which brings me to another point. Although there is comparatively little direct description of sexual encounters in the stories and what there are are largely romanticised, the whole Elric saga has, in its choice of situations and symbols, very heavy sexual undertones. This is true of most Sword-and-Sorcery stories, but I have an idea that I may be the first such author to understand his material to this extent, to know what he's using. If I hadn't been a bit fed-up by the big response received by *The Stealer of Souls* (magazine story, not the book) I could have made even greater use of what I discovered.

Other critics have pointed out the close relationship the horror story (and often the SF story for that matter) has with the pornographic story, so there's no need to go any deeper into it here.

The pornographic content of the Elric saga doesn't interest me much, but I have hinted at the relationship between sex and violence in several stories, and indeed, there are a dozen syndromes to be found in the stories, particularly if you bear in mind my own involvement with sexual love, expression in violence, etc., at the time the stories were first conceived. Even my own interpretation of what I was doing is open to interpretation, in this case!

The allegory goes through all ten stories (including *To Rescue Tanelorn* which did not feature Elric) in *Science Fantasy*, but it tends to change its emphasis as my own ideas take better shape and my emotions mature. When, in the last Elric story of all, the sword, his crutch, *Stormbringer* turns and slays Elric it is meant to represent, on one level, how mankind's wish-fantasies can often bring about the destruction of (till now at least) part of mankind. Hitler, for instance, founded his whole so-called "political" creed on a series of wish-fantasies (this is detailed in that odd book *Dawn of Magic*, recently published here).

Again this is an old question, a bit trite from being asked too often, maybe, but how much of what we believe *is* true and how much is what we *wish* were true. Hitler dreamed of his Thousand Year Reich, Chamberlain said There Will Be No War. Both were convinced—both ignored plain fact to a frightening extent, just as many people (not just politicians whose public statements are not always what they really believe) ignore plain facts today. This is no new discovery of mine. It is probably one of the oldest discoveries in the world. But, in part, this is what nearly all my published work points out. Working, as I did once, as editor of a party journal (allegedly an information magazine for party candidates) this conviction was strengthened. The build-up of a fantasy is an odd process and sometimes happens, to digress a bit, like this.

The facts are gathered, related, a picture emerges. The picture, though slightly coloured by the personalities of the fact-relaters, is fairly true. The picture is given to the politician. If the politician is a man of integrity he will not deliberately warp the facts, but he will present them in a simplified version which will be understood by the general public (he thinks). This involves a selection, which can change a picture out of all recognition, though the politician didn't deliberately intend to warp the facts. The other kind of politician almost automatically selects and warps in order to prove a point he, or his party, is trying to make. So the fantasy begins. Soon the real picture is almost irrevocably lost.

Therefore this reliance on pseudo-knowledge which seems to prove something we wish were true, is a dangerous thing to do.

This is one of the main messages of the Elric

series, though there are several others on different levels.

Don't think I'm asking you to go back over the stories looking for these allegories and symbols. The reason I abandoned *The Golden Barge* was because among other things it wasn't entertaining. The Elric stories are meant to entertain as much as anything else, but if anyone cares to look for substance beyond the entertainment level, they might find it.

One of the main reasons, though, for taking this angle when Alan (Dodd) asked me to write a piece on Elric, was because I have been a little disappointed at the first book being dismissed by some professional critics (who evidently didn't bother to read it closely, if at all) as an imitation of Conan. When you put thought and feeling into a story—thought and feeling which is yours—you don't much care for being called an imitator or a plagiarist however good or bad the story. Probably the millionth novel about a young advertising executive in love with a deb and involved with a married woman has just been published, yet the author won't be accused of imitating anyone or plagiarising anyone. It is the use to which one puts one's chosen material, not that material, which matters.

SOJAN
THE
SWORDSMAN

ZYLOR

The World Of
SOJAN SHIELDBEARER

J. CAWTHORN
R. LUMLEY

1. Daughter of a Warrior King

A MYAT trotted peacefully across the broad, seemingly never-ending plain which made up the landscape as far as it was possible to see. No sound issued from the cloven hoofs, muffled by the moss-like substance which clothed the ground in a mantle of vivid colour—purple, green and yellow, with a trace of crimson or violet here and there. Nothing grew upon that plain. It was a wilderness, barren, deserted—the greatest desert on the planet of Zylor.

A wandering warrior sat astride the myat's broad back. At his steed's side hung a shield, a virtually unknown accoutrement on Zylor, but the tribe to which Sojan belonged had perfected it as a valuable asset. The beast upon which he rode was a big, sturdy animal. From both sides of its huge head grew long sharp horns, curving outward. More like a reptile than a mammal, its head tapered like a snake's, its tail was thick and it, too, tapered.

Sojan was clothed in a bright blue jerkin reaching to his knees, his legs were bare and tough boots of myat hide were upon his feet, reaching to about two inches from his knees. Over the jerkin was a leather harness of simple design—two straps across his shoulders, coming to the waist and attached to a broad belt whereupon hung his weapons—a sword, a dirk, long and sharp, and a holster containing his big, round-butted air-pistol.

The mercenary's hair was long and held by a fillet of leather. At the back of his big saddle were two saddle-bags, a container of water and, rolled across these, his crimson cloak.

The man himself was tall, broad-shouldered and slim-waisted with smooth muscles rippling beneath his jerkin. The perfect fighting-man, keen-eyed and wary.

Suddenly Sojan caught a flash of marble to the west and knew that he had sighted Vermlot, the capital city of Hatnor, the greatest warrior nation of a warrior world. A rich city, was Vermlot, rich in fighting-men and weapons of war, rich in terms of gold, rich in beauty and splendour.

As he neared the city walls a guard bade him halt and state his business.

"I come in peace," he cried, "to offer my sword, my loyalty and my life to his Imperial Highness, the War Lord of Hatnor. I am a mercenary, my only possessions are the clothes I wear, the weapons I carry and the myat I ride. I have travelled half a world to offer my services to your ruler!"

He was admitted to the city and made his way to one of the many taverns situated within the protection of the mighty walls. His strange protective weapon aroused much interest. A certain warrior made mock of him and his shield.

"Oh!" he laughed. "What a brave mercenary! He has travelled half a world—to give us his protection—for with his great shield in front of him he will be able to withstand all our enemies. Perhaps he cannot fight without it. That's so, is it not, mercenary?"

Sojan halted, and gazed up at the man who was leaning against a pillar on the balcony above.

Grimly, quietly, he spoke, but his tones were cold and his words were acid.

"I do not like your attitude," he said. "And I like your words less. Draw your sword—if you know how to use it—and defend yourself! Perhaps you will be hiding behind the shield before I have finished with you!"

The warrior stiffened and his face flushed: he put one hand on the balcony rail and vaulted into the street below, drawing his long "vilthor", a sabre-like weapon, as he did so.

Sojan unslung his shield from the myat and drew his own long blade. The warrior of the Palace struck first, aiming a wicked slash at Sojan's legs with his curved vilthor but the mercenary from Ilthoth jumped high in the air and attacked the other with a weaving arc of steel, driving him further and further back. Then the man saw his chance and slashed at an exposed limb of the mercenary's, but was too slow. There was a dull thud as the sword hit and rebounded from the shield, then he was made to duck beneath a vicious slash from Sojan.

The Vermlotian slowly lost ground until with a flick of his wrist Sojan disarmed his opponent. Then, from a second-storey window a figure dropped, first to the balcony of the first-storey and from there to the ground. He removed his cloak and, with a smile upon his lips, came forward with drawn sword.

"I fancy you will not disarm me so quickly."

This time Sojan was not so lucky for the new-comer was as quick as the proverbial cobra. His sword weaved an invisible circle around Sojan's guard and the newcomer soon had him at his mercy. Before he knew it, the mercenary's sword flew from his grasp and clattered to the earth, ten feet away.

"Yield?" questioned the victor.

"I yield," panted he. "You are a great fighter. Who are you, sir?"

"Perhaps you *have* heard of me," smiled his late adversary, "I am Nornos Kad, War Lord of the Imperial Empire of Hatnor!"

"Sir," said Sojan with a bow, "I, who came to enlist in your service and offer my aid to you, begin by fighting you. I crave your forgiveness."

Nornos Kad laughed. "Never mind, you did very well against my warrior here. To best him is a test indeed and I feel that I would do well to enlist your services." He signed to a servant who was waiting in a doorway. "Come, you will be my guest until I have need of you. Here, Oumlat, take Sojan to one of the best guest rooms and see that he is well looked after."

For a week or so Sojan enjoyed the privileges of the Royal Guest until one morning a messenger came to say that Nornos Kad had asked for him.

"I summoned you, Sojan," Nornos Kad said, when they were alone, "because you are to accompany me on a journey. Our mission is to take Il-that, princess of Sengol, back to her father's country. I desire to bring Sengol into the Hatnorian alliance without bloodshed if possible and the king would think well of it if his daughter was personally escorted home by the War Lord himself. You had better prepare your weapons and be ready to move from your quarters by dawn tomorrow."

Ten warships, heavily armed with Hatnorian air-guns which worked on the simple principle of compressed air, with a range of over half a mile, and the Royal Airship, were ready to take to the air early the next morning. They rose majestically, hovered for a few moments, and then, with motors purring, the great gas-bags veered off towards Sengol which lay far to the north.

Within three or four hours they had crossed the outermost boundary of Hatnor and her satellites and were winging their way at a steady eighty miles an hour over Veronlam, a country which owed no allegiance to Hatnor and which, although fearing the mighty Empire, was constantly stirring up petty strife between the minor Hatnorian nationals. They had nearly reached the border of Veronlam when the soft purr of motors was heard and a shell whistled past them and exploded in their rear air container.

"Veronlam pirates!" yelled the fore-gunner.

Quickly the small fleet formed a protective barrier about the Royal ship. One airship was hit a dozen times in as many different places and hurtled downwards, flames roaring from the gas-bag and the crew jumping overboard rather than die in the flames.

Nornos Kad realised at once that to fight against so many would soon end in disaster for his fleet, and he ordered them to turn about and flee back to Hatnor. He decided to rely upon his speedier engines to aid them rather than their powerful guns.

The Hatnorian fleet circled and fled. Nornos Kad was the last to leave the battle and hastily turned about to follow his ships. But alas, it was too late, for three well-aimed shots in their main tank sent them spiralling slowly to earth to land with a sickening crash amidst a tangle of red-hot girders and flaming fabric. Being on the platform of the ship

Nornos Kad, Sojan and Il-that were flung clear of the main wreckage, to lie stunned.

Sojan did not know how long it was he lay amidst the wreckage of the Royal Airship, but when he awoke it was dawn. He knew that none could have escaped if they had been trapped in the wreckage but nevertheless he spent a fruitless two hours searching for his companions—all he found were two or three charred corpses but none lived. Convinced that his companions were dead he took the only unbroken water bottle and set off in the direction of Hatnor. Sojan's eye caught the gleam of white stone far to the south of his position. With a sigh of relief he began to walk quickly towards the gleam which grew soon into a patch and from that into a city, its walls towering fifty paces in places. Knowing that he was still probably in Veronlam he knew that it would be useless to try to gain admission on the strength of his allegiance to Nornos Kad the War Lord. Stripping himself of his Hatnorian Navy-Cloak and also his Navy-type gauntlets he stood arrayed as when he had first entered Hatnor, as a mercenary swordsman.

He easily gained admittance to the city of Quentos as mercenaries were always welcome to swell the ranks of any army.

"By Mimuk, friend, you're the third to pass through these gates this day," the guard said, as he was allowed to enter the city.

"The third. That's strange is it not, guard?" replied Sojan. "Three people in one day! Mimuk, you must be joking!"

"I joke not, friend mercenary, strange as it seems two others have preceded you and one of them was a woman. Our warriors found them near the wreck of an airship. Some say the ones we captured were Nornos Kad himself and Il-that, daughter of Hugor of Sengol. Two prizes indeed if it be the truth."

Sojan strode off in the direction indicated by the friendly guard.

Arriving at the tavern he hired a room and ordered himself a meal. Finishing his repast, he was horrified to find that the only money he had was that of Hatnor. If he tried to pass this he knew that the suspicions of the keeper of the tavern would be instantly aroused. What should he do? He had brought nothing with him to the tavern save his sword, shield and poinard and the clothes he wore. He reasoned that the only chance he stood was to try and slip quietly out of the door before the proprietor spotted him and ordered him to pay his bill.

Just as he thought he had reached the safety of the street a hand fell on his shoulder and the leering face of the landlord was brought close to his.

"Going so soon, my lord? Methinks you would like to stay and sample some more of our victuals before you make your—er—*hasty* departure," he said with ponderous sarcasm. "Now pay up or my men'll make sure you pay for your meal—in blood!"

"You threaten me, by Mimuk!" cried Sojan, his easily roused temper getting the better of him. "You dare threaten me! Draw your weapon!"

"Hey, Tytho, Zatthum, Wanrim—come and save me from this murdering bilker!" cried the keeper of the tavern in terror.

Instantly three ruffians appeared in the narrow doorway and, drawing their blades, rushed at Sojan, causing him to release his grasp upon the unfortunate man and turn to face this new danger.

Zatthum went down in the first minute with an

inch of steel marking its path through his heart. The remaining two were not so easily defeated. Back and forth across the narrow street the three fought, sparks flying from their blades, the clang of their weapons resounding upon the rooftops. Sojan was marked in a dozen places, but his adversaries were bleeding in as many as he was. With a quick thrust, a parry and another thrust the mercenary succeeded in dispatching the second man. Now only Tytho was left. Sojan allowed himself to be headed off and the man edged him completely around so that they were now retracing their path. With a mighty effort Sojan, who was still tired after his narrow escape from the airship, gathered his remaining strength together and made a vicious lunge in Tytho's direction. He cried out in pain when Sojan's blade found the muscles of his left arm, but did not relax his grip upon his own sword. Again Sojan was forced further back towards the gaping crowd which had collected outside the tavern. His shield saved him from the thrust designed to end the fight but he knew he could not last longer for he was rapidly tiring. Suddenly his foot caught in the trappings of one of the dead men's harnesses and he fell backwards across the corpse. A grim smile graced Tytho's face as he raised his sword to deliver the final thrust.

"Kill him, Tytho, kill him," the crowd roared in frenzied bloodlust.

Sojan, entangled in the harness of the man he had slain, tried to rise but was stopped from doing so by a shove from Tytho's booted foot.

The hireling raised his sword again and the crowd leaned forward.

Suddenly there was a disturbance at one end of the street and the crowd quickly began to disperse.

As it did so, Tytho saw the City Patrol, scourge of the city thieves, was the cause of the crowd's disappearance. Looking hurriedly about him for a way of escape he found none; he dropped his sword and began to run, foolishly, *along* the street.

The leader of the Patrol raised his pistol. There was the slight hiss of escaping air and the running hireling gave a short cry, threw up his arms, stumbled and dropped on the cobbles of the street.

"What's happening here?"

By this time Sojan had disentangled himself from the harness of his late opponent and was standing, legs a'sprawl, hand to head.

"You've saved my life, sir!" he gasped. "These ruffians attacked me for my money. I succeeded in killing two but unfortunately became tangled up with this fellow." He indicated the body. "Tytho was about to finish me when you arrived!"

The leader laughed. "You certainly accounted very well for yourself," he said, "these three are among the worst of the type with whom we have to contend. Ruthless murderers, perfect swordsmen." Again he laughed. "Or almost perfect. You did us a service and I am grateful."

He surveyed Sojan's bloodstained and tattered clothing.

"You're a stranger here are you not?" he enquired. "A mercenary swordsman, perhaps?"

"Yes, I am named Sojan—they nickname me 'Shieldbearer' as I use this." Sojan pointed to his shield.

"Well, Sojan Shieldbearer, how would you like to bear a shield and wield a sword in the Patrol?"

Instantly Sojan saw his chance. If he could get a

post in the organised militia of the city, he might be able to contact his prisoned friends.

"It has always been my ambition to serve in the Veronlamite Guard," he lied, "but to become a member of the great Patrol is a chance for which I had not dared hope."

"Then come with us and we'll enlist you immediately. And," he added, "get you a decent jerkin and harness."

Before he could become a full-fledged Patrolman, Sojan had to undergo a course of basic training. When this was finished, his duties were to Patrol, with his men, a certain section of the city, and arrest any thieves, footpads or similar wrongdoers. The "justice" was rough indeed and was not appreciated by the population. All the time he heard rumours and from these rumours he gleaned that Nornos Kad and Il-that were imprisoned somewhere in the Prison of Zholun—a mighty towered building situated near the centre of the city. Sojan knew well that the Patrol's duties included patrolling the prison and acting as guards to "special" prisoners—and he was hoping that he would be given this assignment soon.

Sure enough, one day his hopes were fulfilled and he was assigned to guard a section of Zholun Prison.

With his eyes wide open, Sojan learned where the two were imprisoned.

"One is in the East tower—the other in the West. Nornos Kad lies in the East tower," a guard told Sojan one night after Sojan had plied him with enough ale to get him drunk.

Sojan had to work fast; there were rumours that his friends were to die by the sword in two days' time.

His first loyalty was to Nornos Kad. He contrived

to enter the East tower wherein Nornos Kad was imprisoned. Stealthily he made his way to the metal-studded door of the cell.

"Nornos Kad," he whispered.

He heard the rattle of chains and through the bars of the door saw his chieftain's handsome face, drawn and pale through lack of food and sleep.

"Sojan!" exclaimed the War Lord. "I thought you died in the crash!"

"I am alive and here to save you if I can. I was assigned to guard the West wing so it will be more difficult—however I shall try and get the keys. Until I return—have hope!"

And with that Sojan crept back along the gloomy passage. On return he found that the Patrolman on duty was talking to someone. He waited until the man had left and then walked into the little room which was being used to house guards.

"Hullo, Stontor," cried Sojan, "what's up?"

Stontor looked worried. "It's my wife, Sojan, she's been taken ill and I can't leave my post."

Sojan saw his chance.

"Well, you go and help her," he said. "I'll stay here until you get back. Don't worry."

"Thanks a lot, Sojan, you're a friend indeed. Here are the keys—shouldn't think there'll be much doing tonight." And with that he picked up his cloak and ran down the long passage.

Hastily Sojan picked up the keys and ran back to Nornos Kad's cell. Unlocking the door he helped Nornos Kad from his chains.

"I was lucky—a coincidence—guard's wife ill—but the main trouble will be getting out of the city," he panted, as he unlocked the heavy padlocks.

Together they returned to the guards' room. Here

Sojan left Nornos Kad. Then he made his way back to the West wing where it was a simple matter to get the princess from her cell Silently they returned to Nornos Kad.

Keeping to the sidestreets and the shadows, the three sped along towards the city gates.

Suddenly Nornos Kad hissed, "Stop! Stop, Sojan, there may be an easier way." He pointed to a flat area dotted with hangers and anchored airships. 'With one of those we would have a better chance of escaping."

"But how?" enquired Sojan.

Again Nornos Kad pointed. "You see that small ship nearest to us—the one anchored down by a couple of ropes?" The ship of which he was speaking was fifteen feet above them, held to the ground by anchors attached to heavy ropes. "With luck we could gain the ship and climb the ropes."

Stealthily they padded along the side of the field, keeping well into the shadows all the time. A single guard lolled on the ground. Sojan crept behind him and reversing his pistol, knocked the man unconscious.

With Sojan's and Nornos Kad's help, Il-that was able to climb the rope and they boarded the ship. As they clambered over the rail a light suddenly appeared from one of the cabins and an armed man appeared on deck. He was followed by three others.

"Mimuk!" he cried. "What have we here?"

There was no time for words and, handing Nornos Kad his long dirk and Il-that his pistol, Sojan drew his sword, and engaged the man and his companions. Nornos Kad was close behind him. Back and forth across the narrow deck the six men fought, and the four crewmen were no mean battlers. Nornos

Kad, weak from his sojourn in Zholun Prison, still put up a good fight. Together they succeeded in killing two of their opponents—but the other two were better swordsmen. The clash of steel echoed across the silent field. Sojan was blinded by the sudden flash of a searchlight and taking advantage of this, his opponent cut past his guard and made a painful gash in his side. The pain was like fire and Sojan could barely restrain himself from crying out He stumbled to the deck and with a cry of triumph the crewman raised his sword. A sudden hiss and a strangled gasp and he collapsed over Sojan. Turning his head he saw Il-that with the pistol in her hand

"Thanks," was all he could say as he struggled to his feet and ran to help Nornos Kad.

While Nornos Kad threw the bodies overboard, Sojan started the engines. Below them they heard shouts of a Patrol and two searchlights were now levelled on the swaying airship. Soon they heard cries as the bodies of the crewmen were found

With two sword strokes Nornos Kad cut the anchoring ropes and the ship rose swiftly into the air There was a coughing roar and the propellers began to turn. The searchlights followed them; all around them shells whistled.

Suddenly, behind them, they saw that three battlecruisers of the fastest and heaviest type had risen to follow them.

"More speed, Sojan, more speed!" cried Nornos Kad. "Make for Sengol, it's nearer."

With a glance at the compass, Sojan turned the ship's nose towards the North. Nearer and nearer came the battlecruisers, guns popping softly. Il-that, a true daughter of a warrior king, climbed into the gunner's rear-seat and aimed the guns of their own ship at the pursuing cruisers. She pressed the triggers and the twin muzzles of the gun gave a jerk, a hiss, and there was an explosion. What all a gunner's skill could not easily have accomplished, Il-that had done with luck—brought down a cruiser in its most vulnerable spot—the main gas-bag. Flames roared from the fabric and the ship lost height. Faster and faster it went as the earth pulled it downwards. The engines roaring to the last it crashed with a flash of orange and crimson flame. But the other two ships had still to be accounted for and Il-that was not so lucky this time.

For two hours the chase continued, neither gaining and all the time the shells from the Veronlam craft were getting closer and closer as the gunner perfected his aim.

"They will catch us soon," cried Il-that, who still sat in the rear-gunner's seat, "they seem to be drawing closer!"

"Then we shall have to land and hope that we're not still in Veronlam," yelled Nornos Kad above the shrieking wind.

"It will be a long time for us to do so, sir," Sojan told Nornos Kad, "we have no anchors, and to release the gas in the gas-bag would mean that while we lost height we should also lose speed."

"Then there's only one thing we can do!" cried the Emperor, "and that's this!" Raising his sword he cut deep into the nearest gas-bag. He was thrown to the deck as the contents rushed out and almost at once the ship began to drop, dangerously fast. The three stood by the side, ready to jump.

With a hard jolt the ship touched the ground, bumped along it, and stopped. Over the side the three companions went and ran over soft moss to

the sheltering shadows of some rocks as the Veronlamite searchlights began to stab into the darkness

But it was easy to hide in the rocks and the caves
sheltered them when the Veronlams landed and made
a vain search for them.

In the morning it was an easy matter to walk to
the nearest Sengolian city and thence to the capital,
where the king gratefully took his daughter and
promised that Sengol would always be an ally to
Hatnor.

(Original draft c. 1955)

2. Mission to Asno

MOTORS PURRING, captains shouting orders, the rustle of the canvas gun-covers being drawn back, gay flags, flashing steel, flying cloaks of many hues; a Hatnorian war-fleet rose rapidly into the sky.

On the deck of the flagship stood a tall, strong figure—that of Sojan, nicknamed "Shieldbearer", second in command to the great War Lord of Hatnor himself—Nornos Kad.

At his side was a long broadsword, upon his back his round shield; his right hand rested on the butt of his heavy air-pistol—an incredibly powerful weapon. Clad in a jerkin of sky-blue, a divided kilt of deep crimson and boots of dark leather, over his shoulder his leathern war-harness, he was the typical example of a Zylorian mercenary, whose love of bright garb was legendary.

The great war-fleet was destined for Asno—a country far to the north of Hatnor where the king, so the spies told, was raising an army of mercenaries to attack Yundrot—a colony of the Hatnorian Empire.

To stop a major war, Nornos Kad decided to send a mighty fleet to crush the attack before it was started.

Having other business, he assigned Sojan to take his place and instructed him to completely wipe out any signs of an attack.

Only too pleased at the chance of battle, Sojan had readily assented and was now on his way—the entire fleet under his command.

Soon the fleet was winging its way over Asno—a land of snow and ice, fierce beasts, great tracts of uninhabited icefields—uninhabited, that is, by *civilised* beings.

In another hour it would be over Boitil, the capital city.

"Gunners, take your positions!" Sojan roared through cupped hands and picking up a megaphone—for there was no radio on Zylor—shouted the same orders, which went from ship to ship until every gunner was seated in his seat, guns loaded and ready for firing.

"Drop two hundred feet!" Sojan roared again to the steersman, and repeated these orders to the other captains, who in turn shouted them to their own steersmen.

"Prepare hand weapons and fasten down loose fixtures, check gas-bag coverings, every man to position!" Sojan shouted when the ships had all dropped two hundred feet.

"Slow speed!" The ships slowed into "second-speed."

In Zylorian naval terms there are five speeds: "Speed No. 1" is fastest possible, "Speed No. 2" is a fifth of this slower, and so on. When a commander gives the order to slow when travelling at Speed No. 1, the ship automatically adjusts to Speed No. 2; if going at No. 2 and told to slow, it changes to No. 3.

Now they were over the outskirts of the city, dropping lower and lower until Sojan thought they would touch the very towers of Boitil, scanning the squares and flying-fields for signs of the army. Halfway over the city a message was passed to Sojan that a great army camp had been spotted—just on the outskirts of the city. At the same time someone yelled for him to look, and doing so he saw that a fleet almost as large as his own was rising from flying-fields all over the vast city.

"Prepare for battle!" he shouted.

As one, the safety catches of the guns were pushed off.

"Shoot as you will!" Sojan ordered.

There was a muffled "pop" and the hiss of escaping air as the explosive shells of the Hatnorian craft were sent on their mission of destruction. Almost at once the enemy retaliated.

Two Hatnorian ships, one only slightly damaged, the other a mass of roaring yellow and blue flame, dropped earthwards.

For twelve hours the great air-battle was fought, developing into ship-to-ship duels as the opposing sides became mixed. Bit by bit the battle moved southwards until it was over the great ice wastes.

But expert handling of their craft, superior marksmanship and a slightly superior weight of numbers on the part of the Hatnorian fleet was slowly but surely weakening the Asnogian fleet. Sojan, now with a gun mounted on the officer's platform, was taking an active part in the battle. His uncanny ability to hit almost whatever he aimed at was taking great toll. Everywhere ships were hurtling earthwards, crashing in an inferno of flame, or merely bouncing gently when a gas-bag was only slightly punctured.

At last, one by one, the enemy began to flee. The other ships, seeing their companions escape, disengaged and followed them. The hired ships, manned mainly by mercenaries, flew in every direction but that of Asno, while the Asnogian craft turned and headed for their home base. In this direction went the Hatnorian fleet, re-forming to a close formation and turning to No. 1 speed. If they overtook a ship it was ruthlessly shot down; but half a dozen or so were lucky and escaped them. In three hours they were back over Asno and bombing the troop encampment with incendiaries until nothing remained of the great camp but smouldering fabric and twisted steel. Through the south gate of the city streamed forth ragged bands of hired soldiers, bent on escaping while they could. The planned attack on a Hatnorian colony had not even begun. A just reprisal on Nornos Kad's part. A reprisal carried out in full by Sojan. But his business was not finished and, landing on part of an undamaged airfield, Sojan ordered the frightened commanding officer to take him to King Tremorn of Asno.

"I bring a message from my Emperor!" he cried when he was in the vast chamber which housed the king's court. All around him stood courtiers and servants, worried and anxious to hear his terms. Great pillars supported the roof and brilliant tapestries hung from the ceiling. Murals on the walls depicted scenes of battles, on land, water and in the air.

"Speak your message," ordered the king. "What are your terms? I admit that I am beaten! For the present!" he added.

"For all time, sir, while a member of the Nornis

family sits on the throne of Hatnor!" Sojan replied. "Now, do you wish to hear my terms?"

"Speak!"

"The first is that you acknowledge allegiance to Hatnor and pay a tribute of five hundred young men to train in our armies every tenth year. The second is that you disband any army you still have, save for policing your city. On signs of attack, you will notify the Empire, who will come to your aid. As a member of the Empire you will be subject to all laws and trading terms of the Empire and in times of major war shall enlist two-thirds of your fighting strength in the armies of Hatnor and the remaining third if called upon. You will not make war-ships or weapons of war, save hand weapons, for your own use, but all war-ships and arms shall be sent direct to the capital. Do you recognise these terms?"

The king paused and, turning to his *major domo*, whispered a few words to him. The man nodded.

"Yes, I recognise your terms," he sighed.

"Then sign your name and oath to this document and seal it with your royal seal. Upon the breaking of your word, the lapse shall be punished according to the magnitude."

Sojan handed the paper to a courtier who carried it to the king. The act of bowing to a king is unknown upon the planet Zylor, instead the subject places his right hand upon his heart to signify complete allegiance.

So it was that Sojan achieved his purpose. But more adventures were yet to come before he could return to his palace at Hatnor.

3. Revolt in Hatnor

"SOJAN, SOJAN!" the call rang across the clear Zylorian sky as a small scout-ship veered towards the larger warship, the flagship of Sojan, second-in-command to the War Lord of Hatnor—Nornos Kad.

"Who are you?" Sojan's lieutenant roared through a megaphone.

"I bring urgent tidings from the court of Nornos Kad—the land is in turmoil!"

"Come alongside," the man roared.

As the scout-ship drew alongside, an armed man jumped from it and rushed up the ladder to the platform whereon Sojan stood.

"Sojan! While the fleet has been at war, revolution has swept through the land. Nornos Kad has been deposed and a tyrant sits on the throne of Hatnor. There is a price upon your head and upon the heads of all whom you command.

"Flee now, Sojan, while you have the chance. Trewin the Upstart controls the city and half the Empire. The other half is in a state of unrest, unsure whether to support one Emperor or another!"

"I cannot flee while my Emperor rots in chains— tell me, who still cries 'Loyalty to the Nornis family'?"

"None openly, Sojan. A few are suspected, but

they are still powerful nobles and even Trewin dare not arrest them without cause."

Sojan's face became grim and he clenched his hand upon his sword hilt.

"Lun!" he cried. "Order the fleet to turn about and adjust to Speed One!"

A look of surprise crossed his lieutenant's face. "We're not running, Sojan?"

"Do as I say!"

"Turn about and adjust to Speed One!" Lun shouted through his megaphone.

At once the great fleet turned gracefully about and adjusted, speed by speed, until it was flying at maximum speed. There were puzzled looks in the eyes of many of Sojan's captains, but they obeyed his order.

"Tell them to set a course for Poltoon," he ordered Lun. Lun did so and soon every ship was heading south—to the steaming jungles and burning deserts of the Heat Lands.

"Why do we sail for Poltoon, Sojan?" asked Lun.

But Sojan's only reply was, "You will see," and he resumed his earnest conversation with the messenger who had brought him the news.

On the third day they were sailing at No. 1 speed over a vast belt of jungle, seemingly impenetrable. But Sojan's eyes, less atrophied by civilised living, caught what he had been looking for—a patch of green, lighter than the dark green which predominated.

"STOP!" he roared. "Stop and hover—no one is to drop anchor."

The flying machines of the Zylorian nations are usually very similar to our airships. The gondola is supported by steel hawsers depending from the main gas-bag. The propeller is adjustable and can be slung either fore or aft of the ship—it is usually slung aft. They are steered by two methods, a rudder aft plus manipulation of the propeller. A normal sized warship usually mounts five guns—two very powerful ones fore and aft, a smaller one on the captain's platform and two mounted in a platform on top of the huge gas-bag. The gunners reach this platform by means of ladders from the deck to the platform. This position is extremely dangerous and if ever the gas-bag is hit it is unlikely that a gas-bag gunner could ever escape.

The ships stopped as ordered and while they waited, Sojan had his ship drop downwards, nearer and nearer to the little patch of green which became a small clearing, just large enough to land one ship, but for a fleet of over fifty ships to land here was impossible. With a slight bump the ship dropped to the ground and the anchor was thrown into the soft grass. Sojan ordered that the gas-bags be deflated. They could always be inflated again as every ship carried a large supply of gas-cylinders.

Now the ship was only a third of the size and was dragged into the undergrowth which was not at all thick. Sojan told his crew of eight to get to work and chip down all the small growth but to leave the huge forest giants standing. This they did and very soon the clearing widened and as it did so a new ship dropped down until the fifty were all deflated and covering a large area of ground under the trees. The cabins made excellent living quarters so there was no difficulty about housing the men. Rations were also plentiful and a spring of fresh water was nearby.

"I know this part of the country well," Sojan told his men that night, "the inhabitants are for the most part friendly. While they are not civilised, they are not savages and I believe that they will give us some help. But now we sleep and tomorrow we shall rouse the tribes!"

Next morning, Sojan with a small party of his men set off for the village of his barbarian friends.

The chief greeted him warmly and was interested in Sojan's need for soldiers.

"You know me and my people, Soyin," he said, using the nearest Poltoonian equivalent of Sojan's name. "We all love to fight—and if there's a bit of loot thrown in, who's to say 'no'?"

"Then I can depend on you?"

"By all means—I shall form a council immediately and recruit as many of my fellow chiefs as possible. Between us we should muster a few thousand fighting men."

By Zylorian standards, where most nations are comparatively small to Earth nations, a thousand men is quite a large number.

"Then have them ready by the third day, my friend," Sojan replied. "Blood will stain the usurper's robes before the month is gone!"

4. The Hordes Attack

THE DAY of the invasion was drawing nearer and Sojan began to work harder and harder in the training of his barbarian horde—the Poltoonians Spies brought word that there was more and more unrest in the outlying provinces of Hatnor.

"The time is right to strike," Sojan told his captains and the wild chiefs. "We must invade now or our cause will be lost and we will never again have the opportunity to win Hatnor back from the usurper and restore Nornos Kad to his rightful throne!"

His airships, camouflaged by the mighty trees of the steaming Poltoonian jungle, were provisioned and ready to do battle. His captains were word-perfect in his plan of invasion. Everyone had his orders and knew how to carry them out.

A day later a horde, consisting of thousands of mounted barbarians led by Sojan himself, moved towards the North—and Hatnor!

Two days later, the faster moving airships rose into the air like a swarm of hornets armed with stings a hundred times more powerful. As they passed the horde, the ships slowed to minimum speed and followed, flying low, just above them. In another day they would arrive at the boundaries of Hatnor—and blood would run in the gutters of all who opposed them.

Sojan was sure that very little blood would flow as the army would be on his side. It was the criminal population, egged on by an evil and power-mad noble, who had risen and overthrown their Emperor while the bulk of his army was crushing a rebellion in an outer province.

There would always be unrest in any regime. Sojan knew this, but there was no cause for the people to grumble about their ruler. As always, the unrest had been caused by a powerseeker intent on turning a nation into a blood-bath for his own selfish ends.

Now the once happy people groaned beneath the tyrant's yoke, no man, woman or child could count themselves safe from his oppression.

Not only men made up the barbarian army, their maidens rode beside them, armed with knife, sword, shield and spear. In their left hands they carried charm sticks to keep their men and themselves from harm. Most of these girls were extremely beautiful and the armour they wore did not detract from their good looks in any way, rather it enhanced them.

At last they reached the outer boundaries of the Empire and found little opposition here. It would be later, when news of their invasion reached the city of Hatnor, that the fighting would begin. Sojan was finding it difficult to keep the barbarians in order; they had decided that anyone could be slain as long as they got their loot. But after a council meeting with the chiefs he was sure that they would be reliable for a time.

Two days later found them at the gates of Vermlot, gates which were securely locked and guarded.

The barbarians were all for laying violent siege to the place, but Sojan realised that they could hold out for an eternity.

"You are forgetting our ships," he said, "we have the whole of the Hatnorian airforce under our control. They will not last as long as they hope!"

His flagship sailed gracefully down for him and then shot up again when he was aboard. Orders were shouted from ship to ship and the fleet dipped downards towards the great city square. Aboard were hundreds of soldiers, the most reliable of the barbarian horde, and as soon as the ships reached the ground, not without some opposition, they swarmed from the ships and ran to engage the rather frightened militia who barred their way.

Wild cries, strangely woven banners raised against a background of flashing steel and muffled poppings of the airpistols and rifles. It was impossible to use the heavier artillery.

Into the square they poured and soon it was impossible to tell friend or foe as the fighting surged back and forth, spreading outwards into the streets, into the very houses themselves. Attacked from the inside as well as at their walls, the tyrant's men were uncertain whom to attack and while they wavered, the barbarians took the opportunity to batter in one of the minor gateways and clamber over the inner wall.

The streets were slippery with blood, echoing with the ring of steel and the cries of the wounded.

Sojan was in front, hewing and hacking with his great blade, his long hair streaming behind him and a grim smile upon his lips. "To the Palace, to the

Palace," he cried. "Take the Palace or our cause is lost!"

And, like a tidal wave, the army surged over their enemies in the direction of the great Palace. The doors would not open to their thunderous knocking so battering rams were brought in. As the main door flew open, Sojan and his men drew back in horror.

There stood Nornos Kad, their ruler, worn and in rags, a filthy stubble on his face. And surrounding him, a body of Trewin's personal guard. Behind them stood their leader.

"Come another step closer, Sojan, and I'll be forced to kill your precious Emperor!" he called.

Sojan and his men were in a quandary, what were they to do? It was checkmate, if not defeat, for them.

An idea sprang into Sojan's mind.

Aiming a pistol at Nornos Kad, he pulled the trigger. The Emperor fell to the ground with a moan and lay still.

"There, dog, I've done your dirty work for you!" he laughed.

In a rage Trewin fired blindly at Sojan. The Swordsman flung himself to the ground and the bullet whistled by to catch one of his men in the shoulder.

Lifting his own pistol, Sojan fired twice. Trewin, in the act of fleeing up the staircase, flung up his arms and toppled down the great stairway, blood trickling from his mouth. He landed with a thud at the feet of his guards.

With a cry, Sojan, his sword glistening in the light of the torches suspended around the wall, charged for the astounded guards who, without thinking, threw down their weapons and fled.

Nornos Kad picked himself up from the floor with Sojan's help.

"A clever move, Sojan," he grinned, "but it took some clever shooting, too."

He examined the hole which Sojan's bullet had made in his coat.

"It was a minor risk, sir. If I had not taken it, the city would even now be in the hands of Trewin."

"At the moment it seems to be in the hands of your Poltoonian barbarians," laughed the War Lord. "Let us go to the rescue of our fellow countrymen."

Peace had come once more to Hatnor.

5. The Purple Galley

To DESCRIBE the wonderful pageantry, the colours, the races and the myriad weapons which flashed in that great hall would be impossible. The gleaming white stones of the hall, hung with vivid tapestries of red, black, gold, yellow, orange, green and purple, almost reflected the equally scintillating colours of the uniforms and dresses of the men and women who stood before the throne of Nornos Kad.

But there was one uniform missing, one tall figure which should have been there was not, one sword did not flash in the great hall.

And the faces of the nobles were sad—for the missing man was Nornos Rique, Prince of Hatnor—the War Lord's son.

"My people," said Nornos Kad, softly and very sadly, "my son has been missing for thirteen days now and still no news of him or the Princess Asderma. Has anyone *anything* to report—you, Sojan, have you found any traces of my son?"

"No, sire, although I have searched the whole nation. I can only conclude that your son is not in the Hatnorian Empire!"

"Then we must find him, Sojan! Take the men you require—and return with my son! If it is possible then you are the man to find him!"

The sun was just setting when a weary and travel-stained rider guided his myat into the small collection of stone and wooden buildings which was the border town of Erm. He had ridden for days, stopping only to eat and gather a few hours' sleep when he could no longer stay awake. His clothes were good and were mainly made of durable hide. His weapons nestled in well-oiled sheaths and scabbards, his shield was covered with canvas. It was easy to see that here was the typical soldier of fortune—a Zylorian mercenary.

He dismounted at the small tavern and called through the door which was ajar.

"Hey there! Is there a stable for my animal and a bed for me?"

"Yes, my lord," came a woman's voice from the tavern and a girl of about eighteen appeared in the doorway. "Hey, Kerk!" she called. "Fetch a blanket for this gentleman's myat and take him to the stables!"

"This way my lord," said the battle-scarred veteran who came to do the woman's bidding. "What's trade like?" he added with a grin as they neared the wooden building which served as a stable for the beasts of the whole village.

"Not too bad," the mercenary smiled. "As long as men are men and their tempers are the same then I'll never be out of a job. There was an uprising in Hatnor some months ago. That was a good scrap if ever there was one!"

"Aye, I heard about it from another gentleman who came this way soon after it happened. Didn't say much, though—most untalkative type if you ask me! He wasn't a Hatnorian—nor a Northerner for that matter, that was easy to see!"

"What do you mean?" The mercenary was obviously interested; more than casually so.

"He was a Shortani man, you can't mistake'em."

"Shortani's a big continent—did you hear him say what country in Shortani?"

"Wait a minute. I believe he did say something." The old man paused and tugged at his grizzled beard. He frowned, thinking hard. "Yes, I've got it—it was raining at the time. Like it does *most* of the time in these parts," Kerk laughed— "Never seems to stop it don't . . ."

"Yes," the mercenary was impatient, "but what did he say?"

"What? Oh, yes. The country. Well, *he* said, when he got here, that it was 'never like this in Uffjir!' Yes, that was it."

"Uffjir, hmm, that's right on the farthest side of Shortani. And even then he may not have been returning there. It probably isn't anything but it seems strange for an Uffjirian to travel so far from his tropical lands, especially in winter. What did he look like, this man?"

"Oh! The usual type, you know. Small, a bit fat, wore one of them fancy jewelled swords which snaps as soon as you cross it with a good bit of Turani steel. Why, I remember when I was a young'un— that would have been a bit before your time. We didn't have none of them newfangled flying machines in *those* days, I can tell you. *We* had to do all our travelling by myat—or more likely on our feet . . ."

"Yes!" The mercenary was almost crying with impatience by this time. "But can you describe the Uffjirian?"

"Well, he had a *beard* if that's any good. And it was curled up a bit—looked as if he'd put oil on it. Wore fancy clothes, too, no good for travelling but expensive—yes, they were certainly expensive. He was a nobleman by the look of him—hired a whole crowd of the village men and they all went off together somewhere. They ain't back yet."

"Have you any idea where they went?"

"Only the direction. They went off in the opposite direction to the one from which you came. Mounted, too, and although they wouldn't admit it, every one of them has a sword hidden in his blankets. They can't fool *me*, I have to look after their myats!"

The myat had been rubbed down and was in his stable by this time, attended by the two men, one an aged veteran with over a hundred years of fighting behind him and the other equally a veteran with not much more than twenty years behind him. They lived short lives on Zylor for most men died of a sword thrust by the time they were seventy or eighty. Their life span of 120 years was rarely reached.

That night, the mercenary sat in the corner of the tavern, drinking and cleaning his heavy pistol. There were two other visitors at the tavern. A young man of seventeen years or so and his father. They were friendly men and the mercenary and he found mutual ground in that they were both veterans of the Findian/Kintonian wars. The mercenary had fought for the Findians and the man—Orfil—had fought on the side of the Kintonians. But there was no bad feeling between the men for at that time Orfil had also been a mercenary. Now he was a merchant— dealing in precious jewels—and he and his son were travelling to Aborgmingi, a small group of islands in the Shortani Sea. The mining of precious stones was unknown there, he said and he found it worth his while to travel the distance over land and sea to sell them as they obtained prices which were over five times as much as those in Fria, his own country.

"Ride with us," he invited, "there is always a greater amount of safety if there is a greater amount of men and I would be glad of your company."

"I ride towards Shortani," said Sojan, "but whether I shall for long depends on circumstances."

The merchant knew better than to ask what "circumstances" they were for privacy means life on Zylor and those who ask too many needless questions are liable to find themselves in an alleyway keeping close company with a knife!

The three men retired to their respective rooms and the mercenary was glad to get some rest. Wearily he sank on to the not-so-soft bed and lay down to sleep.

In the morning he awoke at his accustomed hour and attempted to rise. He could not, for his hands were bound. He was strapped to the bed and the only thing he could move was his head. Looking down at him with a smile on his face was—Orfil the merchant, and his son. Only his "son" had donned her skirts again and was an extremely pretty girl!

"Well, my nosy soldier, you've put your nose into one game too many this time!" laughed Orfil, who seemed to be enjoying a great joke. The girl behind him was not so amused. Her whole bearing was tense and the hand that gripped the pistol at her side gleamed white at the knuckles.

"Perhaps I should introduce myself," continued the man. "my name *is* Orfil. I am the Captain of the

Spies Guild in Rhan. This lady prefers to remain unknown, although where you're going the gods will know it anyway!"

"You're going to kill me then?"

"Yes."

"And am I permitted to enquire 'why'?"

"Certainly. I am afraid that I shall be forced to kill you—though I regret it, sir, for I like you. You see, you have been enquiring just a little too pointedly to be harmless. I suspect that you are more than a common mercenary—that perhaps you are in the pay of Uffjir—and if this is so, then it will be more of a pleasure to kill you!"

"I am no Uffjirian, you oaf! And I am not involved in any intrigue. I seek my War Lord's son who disappeared some time ago! Think not that I would sink so low as you!"

The smile vanished from the Rhanian's face and his right hand clenched on his long sword.

"Then I am sorry! You see Nornos Rique is in this right up to his lance-tip!"

And with that, he raised his sword. The girl turned away, and just as Orfil was about to deal the death thrust, the door opened slowly and he saw the face of the Uffjirian nobleman. Behind him were half a dozen burly swordsmen.

"Yit take you, Parijh!" cried the spy and then to the girl, "Quick, get behind me and open the window. I'll hold them back. There are myats awaiting!"

And with that he rushed upon the Uffjirian who, for a moment was so taken aback that he could hardly defend himself from the furious attack of Orfil's sword.

"Quick men," he yelled, "seize him, kill him, don't let him escape!" But the narrow doorway would not permit more than one man to enter at a time and Orfil easily pushed Parijh back and swung the heavy bar into position as the door shut.

"No time to slay you now," he panted as he clambered over the window ledge, "perhaps some other time . . ."

The girl had by this time scrambled from the window and was waiting with the myats. The soft thud of their hooves was drowned by the yells of the man from Uffjir and the surly answers of his companions.

Silence fell as the men gave chase to Orfil and the girl. The mercenary still lay strapped to the bed. The door was barred from the inside and he had begun to think that he would soon starve to death when someone knocked on the door.

"*Get me out of here!*" he yelled.

"Is there anything the matter, sir?"

This was too much even for a hardened warrior. "Yes there is!" he roared. "And if you don't let me out right now—I'll tear the place down with my bare hands!" A rather vain boast considering his position.

Murmurs at the door and the retracing of steps down the creaking staircase.

He waited expectantly, hearing occasional voices. Then there were tramping feet on the stairway and in a few moments the door fell inwards, closely followed by two men with a battering log and behind them old Kerk.

"I *said* there was something up!" he exclaimed triumphantly.

It was a matter of minutes to untie the mercenary, for him to gather up his accoutrements, to pay Kerk and to find and saddle his myat. Then he was off, down the long forest track, following the trail of Orfil and his pursuers.

For three hours he followed a trail which was easily found. Once or twice he thought he heard movements in the forest but, although he kept his hand ever ready on his sword, he was not attacked.

Then, just as he turned the bend in the trail, they were there. The Uffjirian's men, lined across the narrow path, swords drawn and pikes at the ready.

But the mercenary was trained to quick thinking and at the same moment as his heels dug into his myat's flanks, he drew sword, unhooked shield and brought his lance to bear as he thundered down upon his foes, his crimson cloak flying behind him like a vampire's wings soaked in blood, and a blood-curdling war-shout on his lips!

Taken aback, they wavered, but at the Uffjirian's shouts behind them, pushed forward to meet the charging lancer. Down went one with a brilliantly tufted shaft protruding from his throat. The lance was wrenched out of the mercenary's hands and his steed reared and snorted, flailing with its cloven hooves. His face was alight with battle-lust, he ducked beneath the guard of another man and dealt him a cut which put him down, shrieking and calling to some unknown god in an agony of death. He whirled his steed about, hoping to gain a little ground by retreating, but it was too late, for he was surrounded by a solid ring of pikes and blue steel. He caught blow after blow on his shield and the flat of his sword. One man lunged upwards with his heavy pike and the myat snorted in pain before his deadly hooves beat the man down.

Leaping from the wounded myat, the lone swords-man found himself surrounded by four of Parijh's men. He bled from a dozen superficial cuts and still he fought with the skill and ferocity of a trained *crinja* cat. Then there was a gap in their ranks and he was through, rushing for a tethered myat twenty yards away.

Howling like were-wolves, they followed him across the glade and reached him just as he cut the tethering rope of the myat with his sword and leaped into the high saddle. They attempted to cut at his animal's legs but a swift arc of blue steel drove them back. As he passed the body of the man whom he had first slain, he stooped and wrenched the lance from the corpse and then he was away, down the long trail in the direction Orfil had taken. All his would-be captors heard was a grim laugh which echoed through the tall trees of the forest.

Turning in the saddle, the mercenary saw them run to their mounts and Parijh come from behind, scolding and cursing—for among other things, the fine beast the mercenary had taken had belonged to the Uffjirian!

And it soon proved its worth for he easily outdistanced them and was again following Orfil's tracks—a trail which was to lead to the weirdest adventure in his whole career.

6. The Sea Wolves!

Two DAYS after his fight with the Uffjirian's men, the mercenary rode into the port of Minifjar in the country of Barj.

There were several ships in the harbour. Merchantmen mainly, but here and there rose the tall prows of warships.

Although their airships are motor-powered, the Zylorians have not found an engine capable of moving their ships, or for carrying them for very far and, since steam-power also is unknown, they still rely on sails and oars for motive power.

Most of the ships were equipped with both sails and oars but two of them were built for sails only. From every one of them, long barrels poked from strategic ports, for it was only a suicidal madman who would sail anything but the calm waters of the Asnogi Channel and the Shortani Sea unarmed.

There was one ship, a galley, which stood out from the others. Its tall prow triumphantly above the rest and its sails and paintwork were predominantly purple. Purple, like black on Earth, is the colour of death on Zylor, so it attracted much attention from the inhabitants of the small town.

The mercenary sought out the only presentable inn and bought a meal and a bed for the night.

As he lugged his equipment wearily up the flight of narrow stairs, he looked up and caught a glimpse of a familiar face—that of Orfil of Rhan's girl companion.

Evidently she had been watching him and the warrior kept a wary hand on his sword and resolved to make sure that his door was firmly barred that night.

But soon after he had dumped his belongings on the dirty bed, he heard the rattle of harness and, from his small window, he saw the spy and the girl leaving the walled entrance to the inn—they had none of their possessions with them which told the mercenary a great deal. They had gone for reinforcements. He sat on the edge of the bed pondering what he should do.

He had decided that it would be wiser to leave, when there came the sound of myat's hooves and a squad of Barjite Cavalry, fully armed with lances, swords, long rifles and pistols, clad in uniforms of blue, red and green with shining breastplates, helmets and leg greaves of bright steel. They clattered to a halt outside the inn.

"Thank Yit!" the mercenary murmured. For he recognised the captain of the mounted men as an old friend, who had fought beside him in an expedition Barj had made when bandits had been raiding their caravans of merchandise.

"Red," he cried, opening the window. "Red, you son of a *crinja* cat!"

Red, or as his men knew him, Captain Jeodvir,

Vollitt's son of Chathja, turned. Then, as he saw who called him, a wide grin took the place of his previously astonished expression and he passed a hand through the shock of hair which gave him his nickname.

"Sojan! What are you doing in this particular bit of Hell?"

"And you? One of King Vixian's crack lancers commanding a coast patrol!"

'The king doesn't like me any more, Sojan," laughed the warrior. "Not since I pressed for better pay for the cavalry and nearly started a civil war at the last council!"

It was Sojan's turn to laugh. "You couldn't plead for better conditions for the underpaid infantry, I suppose!"

"What? And have them get the idea that they're up to cavalry standard!"

The rivalry between infantry and mounted divisions in Barj was very real and at times became a threat to the internal peace of that nation. The brawls between the better trained cavalry (generally inheriting the right to become an officer) and the recruited infantry were cursed in every town from Erm to Ishtam-Zhem, the capital. But Sojan was not concerned with this, he had an ally now, no need to run, he could stay and fight like a man.

"Looking for a fight, Red?" he said.

"Dying to be killed, why?" enquired Red, using an expression which was currently popular among fighting men.

"Because I have a feeling that we will be in one soon!"

"Good, I'll tell my men to be prepared."

"Thanks, I'll need some help, I think."

"Unusual for you to admit *that!*"

"Shut up, I'm coming down."

In the courtyard of the inn, Sojan told Red what he knew about Orfil and what had happened to him since he left the court of Hatnor to search for his ruler's son.

And as he finished, Orfil and a band of some twenty mounted men in seamen's clothes, rode into the courtyard. The captain's squad consisted of ten men—so they were outnumbered almost two-to-one. The seamen had no lances but the cavalry had left their rifles, pistols and lances with their myats' saddles and other equipment. Now they were armed only with long sabres (or *vilthors*) and small battle-axes.

It took Orfil less than a second to take stock of the situation and with a curse, he bore down upon the group, yelling a blasphemous battle-shout so full of evil that it made Sojan's hair tingle. His men followed him, hardened sea-wolves these, all of them by rights fodder for the executioner's axe. Scarred, wild-eyed men in exotic clothes of many hues and nations. Black, green, white and red. From every nation on Zylor, they bore weapons which were equally varied—battle-axes, maces, pikes, hooked swords and broadswords, vilthors and blades resembling scimitars. All were there, and many so strange that they defied simple description.

Sojan blocked Orfil's lance thrust with his own long sword and unslung his shield from his back in a hurry. But not soon enough, for Orfil's lance stabbed again and flung the mercenary backward against a wall. Luckily, the lance tip broke on Sojan's breastplate and Orfil swore to his dark gods as he wheeled his steed about and attempted to cut at Sojan with his broadsword. But now Sojan was up again, back against the wall, shield up and blade screaming as he cut past Orfil's guard.

But Orfil was swept away as the fight eddied back and forth across the courtyard. There, a green man of Poltoon went down with a lancer on top of him, stabbing again and again. Near him a huge red man, bearded, with one of his small horns broken and splintered, staggered towards his tethered steed spitting blood from a punctured lung—he never made the myat. A lancer was crushed by sheer weight of numbers as four howling, long-haired black men from Shortani bore him down and almost tore him to pieces. Everywhere was chaos and Sojan hardly knew who it was he fought, there were so many of them. Finally he singled out another red giant who whirled a shrieking twin-bladed axe around his head and laughed through his black beard all the time. He bled from a flesh wound in his left arm and his face streamed blood from a superficial sword cut, but he never seemed to tire. Sojan caught a blow of the axe on his shield which dented so much that it almost broke his arm. Discarding it he skipped nimbly away from the arc of blood-stained steel, ducked beneath it and ripped upwards with a thrust that caught the giant in the throat and threw him groaning to the cobbles before Sojan lost sight of him as a fresh wave of sea-spoilers pushed towards him.

The war-shout of his people was upon Sojan's lips and it rose above the screams and curses of the men, spurred Red and his men on to greater feats of magnificent swordsmanship until the sailors were driven back. Slowly, very slowly, they gave ground and just as victory seemed in the hands of Sojan and his allies, from the courtyard walls dropped scores of well-armoured axemen.

It was impossible to defend themselves against this sudden onslaught and the last thing Sojan heard as an axe haft fell on his helmet and blackness followed blinding light was:

"Take them alive. They will suffer more tonight!"

7. Sojan at Sea

SOJAN AWOKE with a piercing pain in his head which quickly disappeared. Looking about him he found that he was lying on a comfortable couch in a well furnished room which seemed to have an indefinable "something" wrong with it.

Then he realised what it was. Every article of furniture was clamped to the floor and the windows were small square openings in the walls, just below eye-level.

He was in a ship's cabin. Obviously one of the ships in the harbour—that was why the men who had attacked him had worn seafaring garb. Which ship though? He didn't know. Doubtless he would find out soon enough. Could it be the purple ship of death which swayed at anchor in Minifjar harbour? It was likely, this business was mysterious enough for anything.

He walked over to the port hole and looked out. No, the purple ship could be seen from there. Then what ship was this?

He went back to the couch after trying the door which he found locked as he had expected.

He waited an hour—a long hour—until the bar on the door was lifted with a creak and the door swung open.

To his surprise, he found himself staring into the face of Parijh, the Ufffjirian who said:

"Welcome aboard the *Sea Crinja* my friend!"

But the man who stood behind Parijh caught the adventurer's attention most of all. It was his War Lord's son, Nornos Rique of Hatnor!

"Shiltain!" swore Sojan when he saw him. "What—?"

"Explanation later, Sojan, we were lucky to rescue you. Right now you're not very welcome. My fault, I suppose, for giving no hint that I would be going—but there was no time."

"But how did I get out of Orfil's hands?"

"It's a long story—too long to relate here. Meanwhile, we sail for the Sea of Demons!"

"What?"

"We're sailing dangerous waters Sojan, for we play a dangerous game in which the whole planet is at stake. Do you want to come on deck?"

"Thanks."

The three men climbed the long ladders to the poopdeck. Nornos Rique shouted orders as sails were set and men moved to their oars. All the men were well built fighting men.

Sojan looked back to where the huge purple galley swayed at anchor like a dead ship becalmed in the terrible weed jungle of the Black Ocean. She gave no signs of following and soon the sails were billowing, oars creaked in unison and they were on the open sea, bound for the mysterious Sea of Demons.

Like all ships, there was continual movement aboard. Men scurrying up and down the rigging, guns oiled and cleaned, the shouts of the mate giving orders.

The ship comprised three decks. Two raised fore and aft and a middle deck which was little more than a raised platform over the oarsmen's pits on port and starboard. In the centre of this deck there was another slightly raised platform measuring about thirty feet upon which was the single mast. At the base of this mast a drummer sat—beating out a steady rhythm which was followed by the oars who took their timing from the drum.

On this platform, also, was the heavy artillery and something which Sojan had never seen before— harpoon guns, twelve of them, five a side and another two fore and aft.

It was obvious that peaceful trading with the tribes along the Shortani coast was not the object of this particular voyage.

Suddenly, Sojan remembered his comrades.

"What happened to my friends?" he asked.

"They're all aboard the *Purple Arrow*, that cursed ship of Death you saw in Minifjar harbour," answered Rique. "You see, Sojan, we only had time to free you before we were discovered. My men and I swam across and boarded her silently last night. We finally found you and, judging by your snores, you were in a drugged sleep. There were four others with you but they were so much dead weight that we could only take you and secretly leave knives in their shirts with which to aid themselves if they have the chance. I'm sorry, Sojan, but it is too late to go back for them now even if it were practical."

"You are right, of course, Rique," answered Sojan, "but I would that I could help them!"

Now the tall *Sea Crinja* was in open waters, beyond

sight of land. Bound for the terrible Sea of Demons where few ships ever sailed—and returned. And, in the days they sailed towards their destination, Sojan pieced together the ominous tale of the Old Ones and how the Priests of Rhan sought to conquer Zylor with their evil aid.

It seemed that word of the plot was brought to Uffjir first. This country lies due North of Rhan on the Shortani coast and is generally better informed about the island of Mystery as it is sometimes called than is the rest of Zylor.

The Uffjirian monarch, King Ashniophil, had feared to make public the news as it would very likely force the Rhanian priesthood into swifter action. Instead, he had sent a messenger to enlist Nornos Rique's aid as, if the worst ever happened, Hatnor was the most powerful country on the whole planet. Nornos Rique, naturally, had not thought it wise to notify his father at once as he knew the other's aptitude to make quick, but sometimes hasty decisions and this is what Uffjir was trying to prevent.

Unfortunately, at the time of the messenger's coming, the Princess Asderma had been with Rique and had overheard everything. She threatened to betray Nornos Rique to the Rhanians unless he paid her a fabulous amount of money.

Knowing that even when she had the money, she would be dangerous, Rique decided to go into hiding. He had had to kidnap the girl and ride for Rhan in an effort to come to terms with the rulers or, if this failed, destroy or capture their leaders and their strange unhuman allies.

After several detours, he finally reached Minifjar but not before the Princess had escaped and fled to Orfil who had promptly ridden for Minifjar himself where a ship (one of the purple fleet of the Rhanian Theocracy—or Priest Rulers) awaited him in case just such an emergency as this should occur. The mercenary's questions had aroused his interest when he had overheard them at the inn and he had taken Sojan prisoner. Only to be foiled by the Uffjirian messenger who was acting as a rear-guard for Nornos Rique. The rest Sojan knew.

Now it was a race to get to Rhan first.

8. The Sea of Demons

IT WAS a race to get to Rhan first. The *Purple Arrow* would take the comparatively safe way there by sailing down the coast of Poltoon until safer waters were reached (namely the Poltoonian Ocean) and back to Rhan via these waters.

The *Crinja*, however, would attempt to sail through the Demon Sea, cutting off a considerable part of the distance. They knew little of what they had to fight against. The *Arrow* did not know of their plan and was relying on the greater speed to catch the *Crinja* and either destroy it or beat it to Rhan and have it destroyed then. If the *Crinja* could reach Rhan first, it would have several days start and the fate of the world would be decided in those days. Why the *Arrow* had not sailed earlier, they knew not, but guessed that they were waiting for someone.

It was a day's sail until they would reach the Demon Sea and in that time, Sojan got to know his companions better.

Parijh, the Uffjirian, proved to be a humorous man. Cheerful in the face of every danger they had had to meet. When necessary, he was an excellent

144

swordsman, but preferred to keep out of what he called 'unnecessary brawling'. This often gained him a reputation of cowardliness but, as he said, it was an asset rather than otherwise, for what better opponent is there than the one who underestimates you?

Sojan had to agree with this statement and a strong feeling of comradeship and mutual respect grew between them as they sailed ever nearer to the Sea of Demons.

Nornos Rique himself captained the *Crinja*. Rique was a tall man with a face that, though not handsome, had a dependable and rock-hard ruggedness and eyes of steel grey.

The mate was, as is usual on Zylorian naval craft, either privateer or part of an authorised Navy, a cavalry captain by the name of Andel of Riss who, although inclined to make independent decisions without consulting anyone first, was a good man in any kind of fight, and worth four of any man in the crew, who were all fine men and who admired him and respected him as only seamen can respect a man. They would also prove this in a fight with man or the elements.

The custom of placing cavalry men as seconds-in-command of ships is not as strange as it seems and the custom evolved thus:

At one time in the not-so-ancient history of Zylor a strong rivalry developed between seamen and landsmen. It became so bad that if a war came, the land forces could never rely on the naval forces— and vice versa.

It was the idea of assigning landsmen to learn the ways of the sea and naval officers to get to know the cavalry and infantry that saved them from chaos, and nowadays the two forces worked together in perfect harmony.

Later, on the evening of the third day out of Minifjar they were sailing a sea which was similar to any other sea but which, according to the maps, was the feared Sea of Demons.

"We'd better anchor here and sail on at daybreak," Nornos Rique decided, and he gave the order to drop anchor. The anchor chain rattled down for several seconds before stopping with a jarring clank.

"Water's too deep, sir! Anchor won't take!" yelled Andel.

"Then we daren't drift. Ship oars and set sail on your course."

"Yes, sir!"

Night fell forming an atmosphere of decay and death which could almost be smelled or touched. But apart from this, nothing happened save a faint scraping from time to time along the side of the boat which was attributed to some heavy sea-weed or a piece of drift wood.

The twin suns rose and the green dawn came, sending shadows and atmosphere scurrying over the horizon. The sea was green and shone like dark jade with some of jade's intangible mistiness.

Oars smashed into it, ploughing it in bright foam-flecked furrows, and the monotonous beat of the drum began.

Sojan and his comrades ate breakfast in an atmosphere of gloom.

"It's this confounded sea!" suddenly roared Andel, rising from his chair and crashing his fist into his open palm. "Yit! By the time this voyage is over, there'll be men's lives lost and most likely we'll all be on the bottom!"

"Calm down, Andel, we'll come to any danger when we get to it," Nornos Rique said.

Andel grunted sullenly and subsided.

Two depressed hours followed until:

"Yit take us!"

This oath was followed by a piercing scream which tailed off into a choking gasp.

The four men rushed on deck. Most of the crew were at the starboard rail, staring downward to where a red foam flecked the white.

"Turn back, sir, you must turn back!" One hysterical seaman rushed towards Nornos Rique screaming

"Calm down, and tell me what happened!"

Fear was in the man's eyes. A terrible fear bordering on madness. He babbled out his tale.

"A—a *thing*,—sir—it crept up on Mitesh and—oh, sir—it grabbed him by the throat and jumped overboard!"

"Is that all?"

"It's enough, sir!" muttered another of the men.

"What did this 'thing' look like? Who saw it clearly?"

"I did sir."

It was the man who had commented a second before.

"Well?"

"It was a kind of green and brown. Scaly. By Yit, sir, it looked like a man might look if his mother had been a fish!"

"You mean this animal was—human?"

"Not *human*, sir. But it had a man's body sure enough. And his face was pointed, like, sir. And his *eyes*—his eyes were green, like the rest of him, and seemed to rot you when he stared at you!"

"All right. Thank you. Take this man below and give him something to drink!"

"Yes sir. Do we turn back?"

"No! You all knew there was danger!"

"Danger, yes sir, but not from—from *devils!*"

"Get below—we sail on!"

Back in their cabin, Sojan spoke.

"I've heard old folktales, Rique, about occurrences such as this one. Now I know why the ancients called this the 'Sea of Demons'."

"Do you think they are—organised in any way?"

"I've never heard of them being anything *but* in large numbers!"

"Perhaps this was a warning, then?"

"I think it might have been."

"We'd better set all guns in readiness. Those harpoons will come in useful. I had them mounted in case of meeting any of those large saurians that inhabit the Poltoonian Ocean. But it looks as if they'll be needed for a different 'game' now!"

The ship's oars began to creak again. But was the beat of the drum less sure? Were the oars a heartbeat slower? It seemed to the men standing on the poopdeck that this was so.

Towards the middle of the day, the atmosphere of death grew and suddenly from the sea on four sides of the vessel the weird inhabitants of the Sea of Demons rose and attempted to board them.

But this time they were ready and the guns sent forth a steady stream of deadly missiles, driving the shrieking horde back into the sea.

"They went quickly enough!" yelled Andel jubilantly.

"Too quickly. They'll be more wary next time and they'll be back at night for sure!"

And night did fall and with it strange sounds which rose from the water and chilled the blood of the men on board.

But this time the crew were prepared and their searchlights stabbed the gloom, picking out the grotesque figures of the sea-people.

The crew moved forward, their yells mingling with the strange hissing cries of the sea-people. Sabres flashed in the searchlight glare and the blood of seamen and the man-like monsters mingled on the deck, making it difficult to get a footing.

The ship was a contrast of glaring light and total blackness. Men leaped from shadow into blinding gleam or disappeared into murky darkness. Men's breath was streaming in the cold night air. Men's battle cries pierced the shadows where light failed. And Sojan and his companions were in the thick of it, their swords lashing this way and that at their inhuman adversaries. Sojan's war-cry spurred on the men and slowly, then swiftly, they pushed them back and the body of the last monster to invade their ship crashed over the rail to splash into the murky waters below.

There was an audible sigh from the sweating men.

"We've pushed 'em back once, lads, and by Yit, we'll push them back from here to Rhan if needs be!" cried Sojan. With the thrill of victory still in their hearts, their pulses tingling with conquest, the men's voices rose in assent.

A brief count found two sailors suffering from wounds where the talons of the sea-people had ripped them, while three more men were missing, obviously dragged down by the sea-people.

"We should reach Rhan in a day," said Nornos Rique.

"Or the bottom," broke in Andel gloomily.

But the monotonous day ahead was broken only by the screaming of sea-birds as they passed the outlying islands of The Immortal Theocracy of Rhan as it was called. This "immortal theocracy" was little more than Rhan itself and a group of four islands inhabited mainly by primitive tribes, most of whom dwelt in the interior anyway and had probably never heard of Rhan

As they neared Rhan, Sojan felt misgivings. Would they succeed in carrying out their plan? Or would their perilous journey be in vain.

It was with these odd questions in his mind that he followed his friends down the gangplank and down a series of narrow lanes to a private house owned by a society known to those few holding positions of trust in the Hatnorian Empire, as the "Friends of Hatnor." These "friends" were generally native Hatnorians carrying forged or, as in some cases, real papers giving assumed names as well as assumed nationalities.

Three long knocks and two short ones three times repeated gained them admission.

As they walked along the narrow corridor to the main living room they began to feel just a little more secure, even though they were deep in the heart of the enemy's city—Jhambeelo.

But as the door swung open and friendly light flooded into the dark corridor they were taken aback!

"Hullo, Sojan," grinned Red. "I don't think I've met your friends?"

"By Yit! Red, how did you get here before us?" cried Sojan.

"Simple. I flew!"

"What? No airship could make the distance."

"You're quite right. I didn't come by airship. Banjar, here, brought me!"

For the first time, the comrades noticed what appeared to be a hunchbacked, rather tall, man with piercing blue eyes and aquiline features. Dark-haired, with a swarthy complexion.

"To snap the bow in half," said Red, using a term common on Zylor which means roughly—"To cut a long story short," "Jik, Wanwif, Selwoon and myself succeeded in staving a rather large hole in the bottom of the *Purple Arrow*. Naturally enough, it was not long before we were beginning to regret this as the water was rising steadily in the hold. Then, as we were all good swimmers, I thought that the only way to escape drowning would be to enlarge the hole and get out that way. So in turns we widened the hole and, with a great deal of difficulty, pulled ourselves under the keel of the boat and up into the open water. We lost Wanwif, I'm sorry to say. He didn't make it. Well, after that we found that we would have been better off drowning in the ship as there was no sight of land. I learned afterwards that we were in the Black Ocean and this didn't help as the stories I've heard of the Black Ocean are anything but cheerful. But believe it or not, after swimming in a Westerly direction for an hour or so, we were picked up by a little fishing vessel, oared only, manned by some natives of Yoomik which is the largest of the Rhanian group next to Rhan itself.

"The people looked after us but soon we got weary of hanging around their village and decided that an exploratory trip into the interior of the island would be the only thing to break the monotony. We trekked for several days until coming upon the village of Banjar's people—the Ascri.

"The Ascri at one time were enslaved by the Rhanian Priesthood and still bear a grievance against them. It was Banjar, who, when he had heard that I believed you were going to Rhan, suggested that he fly me there. We landed at night and made our way here. Banjar's people are advanced in many of the crafts and sciences and they have an asset which helps them tremendously. Show Sojan and his friends your asset, Banjar!"

Banjar grinned and stood up. Unfolding a pair of huge wings.

"My people, I believe, are descended from the ancient winged mammals who used to live on Zylor. Just an off-shoot of evolution, I suppose. But one which has proved of great help to my people who can travel great distances at great speeds and although we are few in number, we can elude any enemies by leaving the ground and escaping that way. As my friend says, 'It is a great asset'!"

Formal introductions were made and food eaten but when this was finished Sojan spoke to Red.

"Have you managed to find out anything which might prove useful to us, Red?"

"I have indeed, my friend, I have found out something which, with your courage and skill and a great deal of luck, will save the world from chaos!"

9. Prisoners in Stone

RED'S PLAN was simple enough. Members of the secret society of the "Friends of Hatnor" had found an
ancient plan of the Great Temple which was both
chief place of worship and the centre of the Priesthood's rule in Rhan. There were three tunnels leading into it. Old sewers, long since disused. Two
were cul-de-sacs, having been walled up. But in the
last, the walling had been a hasty job and the bricks
used to seal it had collapsed. However, these tunnels were still guarded at the other end. Some said
by Palace Guards—but others said simply that they
were guarded by "something". Even if the foe was
human it would take an incredibly brave man to
venture the rotting tunnels.

"Why not an army?" asked Andel. "Surely a great
many men would be safer than one?"

"Safer, yes, but certainly not so secret. Every action we make must not be detected by the Priesthood—otherwise we are lost. We can only make a
very wide guess at what power these Old Ones
wield and it is our aim to stop them using it—not

bring it down upon our heads—and the rest of the world's heads, also."

"I see," said Parijh, "then let me be the one to go. I offer not out of heroics—which are extremely bad taste in any case—but I am more accustomed to stealth than these sword-swinging barbarians with me." He grinned.

"Ho! So that's what we are, are we?" roared Andel. "I'll have you know . . ."

But the comrades would never hear the rest of Andel's forthcoming witticism for Red broke in: "Be a bit quieter, Andel, or you'll have the whole of the Rhanian Soldiery on our heads."

"Sorry," said Andel.

"No," continued Red, "I think Sojan should go. He is better for the job than anyone else. He has barbarian training, he is cat-footed, lynx-eyed and can hear a sword sing in its scabbard a mile away. I think he will succeed in getting through more than any other man in our company!"

"Then it will be I, that's settled," said Sojan with satisfaction. "When and where do I start?"

"You start now, and I will lead you to the entrance of the tunnel. I suggest that you take a rifle, an axe, your shield and your long sword. Half-armour would be advisable, also."

"Then I shall take your advice," Sojan laughed and proceeded to don half-armour. This consisted of greaves for his legs, and a breastplate and helmet.

Then he was ready and prepared to follow Red down winding backstreets to a small turning near the Great Temple. Here, Red lifted a rusted cover to reveal an equally rusted ladder leading down into darkness.

"Good luck!" was all he said as Sojan slipped

down into the gloom and sought about for hand-
and foot-holds on the ageworn rail. Then the lid was
replaced and Sojan found himself in utter darkness.

Down he fumbled, sometimes missing footing
where one of the metal bars had rusted away, once
nearly falling when his groping hand instead of clos-
ing on solid metal closed on damp air. But at last he
was on the uneven floor of the disused sewer, peering into the gloom. He followed the wall along for
what seemed an eon, stumbling over fallen bricks
and refuse. At last he sensed an obstruction ahead
and he unsheathed his sword and felt the reassuring
butt of his heavy pistol in his hand. On he went,
past the fallen wall until—suddenly—there was no
more tunnel. Or so it seemed. His right hand, which
had been groping along the wall touched nothing.
But after the first brief shock he grinned to himself.
This was the right hand turn of the tunnel. Soon he
would meet the Guardians.

And meet them he did for, with a soul-shaking
shriek, two of the mysterious guardians were upon
him. Huge reptilian things, red-eyed and red-mouthed
with teeth reaching a foot long and razor sharp.

Sojan, shocked by their sudden attack, took a step
backwards, hitched his rifle to his shoulder and fired
straight into the mouth of the foremost beast. It
shrieked again but still came on. Hastily he dropped
the rifle and replaced it with his heavy axe and long
sword. But before the beast reached him it had stumbled and fallen with crumpling forelegs, writhing in
a fit of agony which ended with one abrupt shudder
of death.

The other monster was checked for a moment,
sniffed the corpse of its companion and then voiced
another spine-chilling shriek which was half hiss and

half human cry. Sojan met it with sword lashing and axe whining through the air about his head. Back went the monster but it returned in an instant, clutching at Sojan with its claws which almost resembled human hands—though hands with six inch steel talons on the ends of each finger. Sojan stumbled backwards, his axe cutting and hacking at the hideous thing, his sword slashing into its throat again and again until at last it was down in a death agony that lasted minutes.

Pausing to wipe his weapons clean of blood and to pick up his rifle, Sojan moved on down the tunnel, feeling a little more cheerful now that he knew his foe and had conquered it.

And, abruptly, he was at the end of the tunnel and a similar steel ladder, in better condition, leading upwards. Warily he clambered up. Rifle, axe and shield strapped across his broad back and his sword firmly clenched in his teeth.

There was a metal cover here, too, and he lifted it cautiously to be blinded for a moment by the sudden gleam. He had been so long in darkness and the semi-darkness of the tunnel that he blinked hard for several seconds until his eyes became accustomed to the light.

Silently he eased his body through the narrow hole and just as softly replaced the cover. He was in a lighted corridor with torches on either side. The corridor was short and had a door at each end. Which door? He decided immediately to take the door which led farthest away from the tunnel. At least he would be a little deeper into the Temple and nearer the Inner Room in the centre which housed the Old Ones.

Gradually he pushed the door until it swung open.

He thanked the Gods of Light, Yit and Corrunj, that they had not been locked.

Down another corridor he sped, cat-footed as ever, wary hands on sword and rifle. His armour glinted in the torchlight and his shadow loomed black and huge on the wall.

Most of the priests would be at rest, he knew, but it was equally certain that guards would be posted at strategic points and absolute caution was necessary. He had a rough plan of the Temple printed in his mind but the maze of corridors which he was following and which ran deeper and deeper into the heart of the Temple were complicated and were probably or more recent origin, for the map had been very old.

But cautious as he knew he must be he was certainly not slow. For every heartbeat counted. He had to reach the chamber of the Old Ones somehow and discover who—or what—they were and what their motives were for allying themselves with the evil Priesthood of Rhan.

The murmurs of voices. The laughs of men. The clank of sword-scabbard against armour. At last, a guarded entrance. Was he near the strange sanctuary of the Old Ones?

The men's backs were to him. This was not the time for heroics, for a cry would mean discovery; and discovery he must avoid. He raised his rifle and brought it down on the head of one guard while with his other hand he chopped at the back of the other man's neck. They both collapsed without a murmur. Looking up and down the intersecting corridor to make sure he had not been seen, he grabbed the two bodies by their loose clothing and pulled them back into the shadows. No time to hide them. And no time to hide himself. For the clank of steel-

shod feet resounded down the corridor. He hugged
the wall and prayed to his ancient gods that he
would not be discovered.

Sojan heard the steps come nearer and nearer,
and then, miraculously, fade away again. Risking
discovery, he peered round the wall and saw another passageway. Down it strode two guards and
one of the infamous High Priests of Rhan, the rulers
of the place. Cat-footed as usual, he followed them.
This corridor was not very well lighted but, unlike
the others, it had doors set in the walls.

Sojan hoped that one of these would not open.

Suddenly the priest stopped.

"Wait here," Sojan heard him say. No time to
think, now, he must act. Into the nearest apartment
and pray to Yit that it was unoccupied.

Luck! The rooms were empty. These, Sojan could
see, were the apartments of the High Priests. No
monkish sparsity of furniture here—these rooms were
lavishly furnished and decorated. Grinning, Sojan
bounced down on to the bed and breathed a prayer
of relief. Then he was up again and taking in his
surroundings. On one wall hung several of the long
flowing robes which the High Priests wore.

One of the customs of these men was to go
veiled—to give them a little more security from the
assassin, Sojan guessed—and also to enable them to
slip from the Temple and mingle with the people
without fear of being recognised. This was one of
the reasons why the people of Rhan were so easily
kept in subjection by the evil priest-Rulers.

But there was a chance, though Sojan knew it was
a slim one, that he could don one of these robes and
enter the Inner Chamber and meet the mysterious
Old Ones face to face.

Quickly he slipped into the robe
his sword and pistol under a nea
hoping that they would not be disco
and pistol were well hidden by the
and he could keep his armour on.

Out now, and down the passage, past the ~~~~~
ing soldiers who sprang to attention and saluted him
with the usual Zylorian salute—clenched fists against
temples and a short bow from the waist.

Sojan acknowledged the salute by a curt nod of
his head. The veil hid his features entirely, and if he
was unmasked by some mishap—only the other High
Priests would know whether he was a fraud or not.
So, comparatively safe, Sojan moved along the corridor towards the huge, metal-studded door which
was the portal to the Inner Chamber.

It was unlocked, and the guards on each side of it
stood away respectfully as Sojan opened it.

At first he could see nothing, the room was lit by
one torch which cast shadows everywhere. Then,
from one corner of the large chamber, a voice spoke.
It was a voice of infinite weariness, full of lost hope
and the knowledge of an eternity of despair.

"Why trouble us again, Priest, we have promised
to do your bidding? And *we* keep our word—if you
do not."

Sojan realised that instead of the evil forces he had
expected, here were prisoners; slaves rather than
allies of the Priesthood.

"I'm no priest," he said, "if I knew who you were
I might help you even!"

"Is this another trick, Priest," murmured the voice,
although this time there was a little hope in it.

"No trick. I'm a sworn enemy of the priesthood of
Rhan. I represent the rest of Zylor, who have no

ecome enslaved by the Rhanians. Yet rumour
that you are allied with them." He squinted
the darkness. "Who are you—or what?"

"We are the old inhabitants of Zylor. We lived
here before ever the shining ships of humanity sprang
from distant planets in a desperate attempt to reach
another habitable planet. They thought that the end
of their world had come. As it happened their world
did not die, but it was too late then, they had taken
all their knowledge out into space with them, and in
the long journey from Galaxy to Galaxy much of
their knowledge perished, for the journey took centuries to complete.

"By the time the new generations reached this
planet, their ancestors had died and Man had to
start again, almost from the beginning. These Men,
who called themselves "Lemurians" lived peacefully
with us for many hundreds of years and we helped
them as much as possible, for we are a very ancient
race and had more knowledge than ever the ancestors of the Lemurians, although of a different kind—
for while Man concentrated on improving his body,
we concentrated on improving our minds and could
control mighty elements with our wills. Eventually
the Men became frightened of us and sent us away
(there were only a few of us living in far-flung colo-
nies then; now we are even less)."

"But how did you become the slaves of these
priests?" asked Sojan. "What happened?"

"Although there were many men who feared us
and called us Things of Evil and similar names, there
were others who began to worship us for our powers, calling us gods and setting up altars and Temples to us.

"Just as some men are foolish, some of our number were foolish and began to think that perhaps they *were* gods after all. They dwelt in the Temples and had sacrifices made to them and took part in meaningless rituals. The priests soon found their weaknesses, however, and decided that they could rule the people if they frightened them by telling them of the wrath of the gods and so on. They succeeded in capturing us and imprisoning us. I was one of the foolish ones, our contemporaries have long since left this planet in search of another, uninhabited by Man, with whom they cannot live in peace.

"You may have read in your history scrolls of the mighty Theocracy which dominated the world at one time. Rhan is now all that is left of the Theocracy—a remnant of a great and terrible nation! The people rose against their oppressors, country by country, until the evil Priesthood was driven back, further and further, to seek refuge on this island, the original capital of the old Imperial Theocracy. It was here that the cult, based on worship of us, was spawned and, if you can help us, it is here that it will die. Otherwise a new Black Age shall cover the world in a cloak of death!"

"But," cried Sojan, "if you do not wish them to rule Man then why do you help them? Why do you lend them your powers to destroy the great Nations of Zylor?"

"They have promised us freedom, O, Man! Freedom after thousands of decades. Freedom after eons of despair. We would follow our brothers, we would travel the infinite lengths of Space and Time were we once released. We would see Suns and Planets, green things. Seas and Plains. For us these things are worth more than life. We are *of* them more than

Man—for we, like the planets and the stars, and the grass that grows for ever, are almost immortal. We have no bodies, as Man knows bodies, no senses as Man interprets senses—we are Minds. You can see that the temptation is great! We were not strong-willed to begin with, we were proud of Man's petty ceremonies. Now that he offers us Light and Freedom again, we *must* accept. Unless there is another way."

"There may be another way," Sojan said. "If you will but tell me *how* you are imprisoned, perhaps I can release you!"

"There are certain minerals, rare and almost unknown, which have the properties that lead has compared to radium. Radium cannot harm or pass through lead. Similarly, although we can pass through most minerals and life forms, we are imprisoned if we enter a certain precious stone. We can enter it, but by some strange trick of nature, our beings cannot pass back through it. Thus we were enticed, centuries ago, into these blocks of *ermtri* stone. The only way in which we can escape is by someone outside boring shafts into the blocks and thus cutting channels through which we can pass. Do you understand?"

Dimly Sojan understood, though his brain was shaken by the effort of trying to imagine beings so utterly alien to Man, yet in some ways akin to him. He picked up the torch and cast its light towards the centre of the hall. There on an altar, covered by a crimson cloth, rested five large blocks of some dark, cloudy blue substance. Like—like blue jade. It was a stone that Sojan, who had travelled the whole of his planet almost, had never seen—had never, what is more, heard of—not even in legends.

"I understand," he said, "what tool will cut it?"

"Steel, sharp steel will bore into it. Have you steel?"

"Yes. Will it hurt you?"

"No, it will leave no impression."

Wiping sweat from his forehead and hands, Sojan moved towards the blocks. He drew his sword and clambered up on to the altar. Placing the sharp point of his blade on top of the first block, he turned it round and round. Feeling it bite deeper and deeper into the strange substance he became aware of a strange tingling which seemed to flow up his sword and into his body, he couldn't define it but it was not unpleasant. Suddenly there was a dazzling burst of green and orange brightness and something seemed to flow from the hole that he had bored, flow out and upwards, lighting the room. He heard no words, but in his mind there was a great sense of joy—of thanks. Then, one by one he saw the other blocks, broken by the same strange power, open and the green and orange brightness flow from them.

Then they took on a slightly more solid shape, until Sojan could make out eyes and circular bodies. These, then, were the Old Ones. Perhaps in a million, million years, man too would have succeeded in being able to form the atoms of his body into whatever shape he desired. Perhaps, these beings once were Men? That would explain the strange kinship Sojan felt for them. A kinship which his Lemurian ancestors felt also, before their witnessing of such alien powers changed their finer feelings into those of fear and hate.

"Before you leave," Sojan begged, "I crave one request as a price for your release."

"Anything!"

"Then when I am out of this building and safely at sea, destroy this place of evil so that the power of the priests will be shattered for all time and such an evil can never rise again!"

"Gladly we grant you this. We will wait here until you are at sea. But tread carefully, we cannot help you to escape."

Thanking them, Sojan turned about and left, sword in hand. But in his exultation he had forgotten the soldiers outside and they stared in amazement at the sword in his hand and the sweat on his face. This did not seem to them any High Priest.

Taking quick stock of the situation, Sojan spoke to them.

"I—I had a little difficulty with one of the bolts on the interior," he lied, "I had to use this sword to loosen it . . ."

With a puzzled look, the men bowed and saluted, but there was doubt in their eyes.

"A priest would not go unveiled for anything," he heard one of them murmur as he entered the room which he had left previously. "He doesn't seem a priest to me! Here you, stop a minute!"

But Sojan had bolted the door and was hastily donning his weapons again. The men began to bang on the door and more men came to see what the noise was about.

"That's no priest," he heard someone say, "The High Priest Thoro is conducting the Ceremony of Death in the Outer Temple! He won't be back for hours!"

"Batter the door down you fools," came a voice that was obviously that of one in authority, probably a High Priest.

Anxiously, Sojan looked for another exit. There was only a curtained window.

He parted the curtain, and looked outside. It was still dark. He looked down. A courtyard scarcely ten feet below. *With luck*, he thought, *I can jump down there and escape as best I can.* He put a foot on the ledge and swung himself over, dropping lightly to the grass of the courtyard. In the centre of the court-yard a fountain splashed quietly—a scene of peace and solitude. But not for long. He saw a face at the window he had so recently quit.

"He's down there," one of the soldiers shouted.

Sojan ducked into the nearest doorway, opposite the room he had left. He ran down a short, dark corridor and up a flight of steps. No sign of pursuit yet. Panting heavily he ran in the direction he knew an exit to be. It would be guarded now, he knew, for the whole Temple was by this time alert. And so it was. With his usual good luck, Sojan had succeeded in making the exit unchallenged. But there would be no such luck here, with five huge soldiers coming at him.

Again he had no time for heroics. His pistol came up and two of his would-be killers went down. The other three were on him now and his sword cut a gleaming arc about his head. His battle-axe shrieked as if for blood as he carried the attack towards his foes instead of they to him. Nonplussed for a sec-ond, they fell back.

That falling back was for them death, for now Sojan had some kind of advantage and he made full use of it as he drove blow after blow, thrust after thrust into the men.

Bleeding himself from several wounds, Sojan came on, down went one man, then another. Now the last warrior, fighting with desperation hacked and parried, and sought an opening in Sojan's amazing guard.

None came, the man sought an opening too often, lunged forward—and almost pinioned himself on Sojan's blade. Back he tried to leap, clumsily. A perfect target for a whistling, battered axe to bury itself in helmet and brain.

Leaving his axe where it had come to rest, Sojan fled the Temple. His heart pounding, he finally reached the house where his friends waited.

"Come," he cried, "I'm successful—but we must make the ship immediately, all of us, else we all die. I don't know what they intend to do."

His companions realised that there was no time for an explanation and followed him wordlessly.

A frantic race for the docks. One brief skirmish with a City Patrol and then they were on board. Up anchor, out oars, castoff.

And as the ship sped from the harbour they looked back.

There came a blinding flash and then a deep, rolling roar as the great Temple erupted in a sudden burst of flame. Then, as they peered back at the city, there was blackness again. The Temple was not burning—there was no Temple now to burn—it had been dissolved.

As they watched, Sojan and his friends saw five streaks of blue and orange flame rise skyward and rocket upwards and outwards—towards the stars.

"What was that?" gasped Nornos Rique.

"The Old Ones," smiled Sojan. "I'll tell you a tale which you may not believe. But it is a tale which has taught me much—as well as giving me a valuable history lesson!"

The voyage back was not a boring one for Sojan's companions as they listened to his strange tale.

But what of the Purple Galley you ask, what of Orfil and the Princess who betrayed Rique? That, readers, is a story which is short and sad. They, too, attempted to sail through the Sea of Demons in pursuit of Sojan and his companions.

But they were not so lucky.

10. The Plain of Mystery

THE WIND tore at the rigging of the tiny air-cruiser as it pushed bravely into the howling storm.

Four men clung to the deck rails whilst a fifth strove to steer the tossing gondola.

"Keep her headed North!" yelled Nornos Rique to Sojan.

"At this rate we'll be tossed on to Shortani unless the wind shifts!" he yelled back.

Parijh the Uffjirian grimaced.

"I've been meaning to go home for some time!" he called.

"You'll be home for your own funeral unless someone gives me a hand with this wheel!" cried Sojan.

Sojan, Nornos Rique, Parijh, Andel and Red, the five men who had saved their planet of Zylor from the evil priest-rulers of Rhan some months ago, were returning to Hatnor after being the guests of honour at several banquets held to celebrate their triumph. Sojan, Rique, Andel and Red had been uncomfortable about the whole thing, only Parijh, always glad of the limelight, had enjoyed himself thoroughly.

The storm had sprung up quickly and they were

now battling to keep the little dirigible into the wind which drove them steadily southwards.

"Wouldn't it be better to land, Sojan?" Andel shouted.

"It would be, my friend, if we knew where we were. There's every likelihood of getting out of this trouble into something worse."

Suddenly there was a loud snapping sound and the wheel spun throwing Sojan off balance and on to the deck.

"What was that?" yelled Parijh.

"Steering's gone! We can't attempt to repair it in this weather. We'll just have to drift now!"

The five trooped down into the tiny cabin. Even there it was not warm and they were all depressed as they shivered in their cloaks and attempted to get some sleep.

Morning came and the storm had not abated. It lasted all through that day, the wind ripping into the ship and sending it further and further South.

"There's never been a storm like this in my memory!" Nornos Rique said.

The others agreed.

"Further North," said Andel, "they're quite frequent. Lasting for days, so they say."

"That's true," said Sojan.

By midnight of the next night the storm finished and the sky cleared of the clinging cloud. The stars, their constellations unfamiliar to Earth eyes, shone brightly and Sojan took a quick bearing.

"We're over Shortani all right," he muttered. "Well over. In fact, I believe we're near the interior of the continent."

Beneath them the scene was one of peace rather than that of death and mystery. Great plains, watered by winding rivers, lush forests, rearing mountains, proud—like gods looking down upon men. Here and there herds of strange animals could be detected for the moons were very bright. They were drinking and did not look up at the airship gliding silently above them.

In the morning Sojan and Andel set to work on repairing the broken steering-lines whilst the others looked down at the peaceful-seeming country beneath them.

All the time they worked they drifted further and further into the interior.

"If we drift much further Sojan, we won't have enough fuel to get us out again. Remember, we only had enough for a short journey!" Parijh called up to him where he was working on the steering gear.

"Yit take us! I hadn't thought of that," cried Sojan. "But there's nothing we *can* do until this steering is fixed. Work as fast as possible Andel or we'll be stranded here!"

But repairing the steering wires and readjusting the rudder, especially sitting in the rigging with only a flimsy safety line between you and oblivion, isn't easy and it took Sojan and Andel several hours before the motors could be started up again.

"There's not enough fuel to make it back to Hatnor," Sojan said. "But if we're lucky we'll make a civilised country on the Shortani coast!"

Now there was nothing they could do but hope and the men relaxed, watching the wonderful scenery beneath them and speculating on what kind of men, if any, lived there.

Red, who played a Zylorian instrument called a *rinfrit*—a kind of eight-stringed guitar, sang them a song, based on an old legend about these parts. The first verse went something like this:

> "There's many a tale that has been told
> Of Phek the traveller, strong and bold!
> But the strangest one I've ever heard—
> Is when he caught a *shifla bird*."

"What's a *shifla bird?*" enquired Andel curiously.

"Oh, it's supposed to be as big as an airship and looks like a great lizard."

His companions were amused at this story, and all but Sojan, who was looking over towards the West, laughed.

"Don't worry too much," said Sojan calmly, "but is that anything like your *shifla bird?*"

And there, rising slowly from the forest, was the largest animal any of the adventurers had ever seen. Earth men would call it a dragon if they saw it. Its great reptilian jaws were agape and its huge bat-wings drove it along at incredible speed.

"It seems there was some truth in the legend," muttered Red, licking dry lips and automatically fingering his pistol at his belt.

"There's always some truth in legends," said Sojan, "however incredible."

The thing was almost upon them now, obviously taking their cruiser for some kind of rival. It was as big as their cruiser although its body was about half the size whilst its wings made up the rest of its bulk. It was a kind of blueish grey, its great mouth a gash of crimson in its head whilst wicked eyes gleamed from their sockets making it look like some supernatural demon from the Zylorian "Halls of the Dead".

"Drop, Sojan, drop!" cried Nornos Rique as the men stood for a moment paralysed at this sight of something which they attributed only to the story scrolls of children.

Sojan whirled, rushed over to the controls and pushed several levers which opened valves in their gas-bag and caused the ship to lose height quickly.

The *shifla* swooped low overhead, barely missing them and causing them to duck automatically. Suddenly there came a crashing of branches, the ripping of fabric and the harsh snap of breaking wood. The ship had crashed into the forest. The men had been so busy trying to escape from the danger above them that they had forgotten the forest beneath them.

Sojan lifted his arm to shield his face and flung himself backwards as a branch speared through the ship as if it were a fish and nearly speared him at the same time. Eventually the noise stopped and, although the ship was swaying dangerously and threatening to fall apart any moment, sending the men to destruction, Sojan and his friends found that they had only bruises and scratches.

Sojan's barbarian instincts came to the rescue. Cat-footed as ever he clambered out of the wreckage on to the branch which had almost killed him.

"Quick," he yelled, "after me!"

His friends followed him quickly, Parijh panting with the effort. They moved cautiously along the branch and finally reached the trunk of the tree. Down they clambered, easily now for the tree was full of strong branches and it was only a drop of four or five feet to the ground.

Sojan looked up to where the airship dangled, its great gasbag deflated, the gondola smashed and torn.

"When that falls," he said, "we'd better be some

distance away for it's likely that the engine will explode.''

''There go our supplies and rifles and ammunition,'' said Nornos Rique quietly.

''We've got our lives—for the present at least,'' Sojan reminded him. ''We'll have to head steadily Northwards and hope that we don't strike a mountain range. If we are lucky we can follow a river across a plain. Several plains adjoin civilised or semi-civilised territories don't they, Parijh?''

''One of them runs into my own country of Uffjir, Sojan, but there's one chance in fifty of making it!''

''Then it looks as if we'll have to chance it, Parijh,'' Sojan replied slowly, looking over towards the East. ''But at least we shall be able to ride. There—see?''

They looked in the direction in which he was pointing. About a mile away, a herd of myats grazed placidly.

''Fan out—we should catch them easily if we organise properly,'' Sojan called.

Slowly, so that they would not disturb the animals, Sojan and his friends closed in on the myats. Once trapped they were easily caught for, unlike most animals used as beasts of burden, myats were bred originally for the sole purpose of carrying man.

Now that they were mounted, the friends made good time in the direction in which they were headed. Some days later Sojan caught sight of a strange gleam in the distance—as if the sun was glancing off a highly polished surface.

''Head in that direction,'' he called to his companions. ''There seems to be a building of some kind over there!''

And sure enough, it was a building. A great glistening domed construction, rising hundreds of feet, so it seemed, into the air. It was built of a similar stone to marble—but what was it? And why was it standing alone in such a savage wilderness and (this troubled the companions more than anything) were there men using it now?

"The only way to find out who or what is in there is to go nearer," said Andel.

"You're right," agreed Sojan. "Let's go!"

They forced their steeds into a quick trot.

They dismounted silently and made their way cautiously to the wide entrance of the place, which seemed to be unguarded.

There were windows high above them, seeming to be set in rooms situated at different levels in the building. Part of the roof was flat but most of it rose in a magnificent dome. Although there were no signs of corrosion at all, the men got the impression that the building was centuries old.

"There seem to be no stairs in the place," mused Sojan, looking around him at the gleaming marble halls which they had entered. To his left were two sheets of shining metal, seemingly set into the walls for no reason. To his right was an archway leading into a room just as bare as the one in which they now stood.

"Wonder what these are?" Red said, brushing his hand across one of the metal sheets.

Instantly there was a faint hum and the sheet of metal disappeared upwards, revealing a small—was it a cupboard?

Red stepped warily into the alcove, sword in hand. At once, the sheet of metal hummed downwards behind him.

"*By Yit. He's trapped!*" cried Sojan.

He brushed his own hand across the metal, but

nothing happened. For several minutes he tried to open the metal door but it seemed impossible. How Red had done it, they could not tell.

Suddenly from the outside came a yell.

Rushing into the sunlight they looked up—and there was Red, looking very cheerful, grinning down on them—from a window of the tenth storey, the one nearest the roof.

"How did you get up there?" called Nornos Rique.

"The 'cupboard' took me up! It's a kind of moving box which lifts you up to any storey you wish. Though I had to go all the way up. There were lots of buttons to press, but I dare not press any of them. After I'd got out, the doors closed again. I tried to get back in but the doors at that end wouldn't move. It looks as if I'm stuck here for life."

He didn't look as if he was particularly worried about the prospect.

Comprehending, Sojan rushed back into the great hall and again passed his hand over the metal "door." It hummed upwards. He didn't step in immediately but waited for his friends to join him.

"The ones who built this place must have been wonderful engineers," remarked Sojan. "And by the way, I recognised the language in which the directions for the operation of that thing were written—it's old Kifinian!"

"What?" exclaimed Parijh. "You mean that the ancestors of the Kifinians built this?"

"Obviously. Otherwise how do you explain the language?"

"From what you learned at the Temple of Rhan, Sojan," mused Nornos Rique, "the ancestors of the entire planet, so far as human beings like ourselves are concerned, came from another planet thousands of years ago—perhaps this was built before the race spread and degenerated. But what could it be?"

"I think I know," answered Sojan. "Notice how the whole area around the building is entirely treeless—a flat plain—a few shrubs, now, and other vegetation, but for the most part flat. This place was a landing field for airships of some kind. We have, as you know, similar landing fields all over the civilised parts of Zylor. This place was a control station probably."

Suddenly Red who had been standing by the window called to his friends.

"*Look, down there!*" he yelled. "*Savages, hundreds of them!*"

Below them swarmed a silent mass of strange near-human creatures. They all carried spears and broad-bladed swords. They were covered in short, matted hair and had long tails curling behind them.

"We seem to have violated taboo ground, judging by their actions," said Parijh who knew the people better than the rest, for his race occasionally traded with them. "They won't enter themselves, but they will wait until we come out—as come out we must, for food."

"The best thing we can do," said Andel, "is to look around this place and see if there is any other way out."

"Good idea," agreed Sojan, "if you see any more of those metal plates, try to open them."

They split up and each explored a certain section of the floor. Soon they heard Andel call from the centre of the building. Rushing to the room from which he had called they were astounded to see a large, opened panel. This one revealed a kind of bridge spanning a drop which must have gone right down to the foundations of the building. The bridge led to a huge, streamlined shell of gleaming metal fitted with triangular fins.

They stepped on to the bridge and moved single file across it until they reached a door. Scowling faintly, Sojan deciphered the ancient hieroglyphics on it.

"Here we are," he said, pressing a button. "To Open." And open it did.

"It's obviously an airship of some kind," said Andel, who was the most mechanically minded of the five. "Probably a ship similar to the ones in which our ancestors came to this planet."

"You mean an airship capable of travelling— through *space?*" said Sojan.

"Perhaps," said Andel, "but also travelling from continent to continent probably. If only we knew how to operate it!"

They finally managed to find the control room of the ship. All around them were tiers of dials and instruments. Working quickly, now that the script was becoming more familiar to him, Sojan deciphered most of the captions on the instruments. Set on the main control panel were levers marked, "Automatic, Emergency, Poltoon, Automatic, Emergency, Jhar", etc. The names were those of continents.

"We can't stay here all the time," said Sojan. "If we stay we will starve to death, if we go outside we die, we might as well risk it." So saying, and without waiting for his friends' advice he pulled the lever marked Poltoon and stood back.

There came a gentle hum as the door through which they had entered closed. Another hum grew steadily louder and the entire roof of the building opened out letting in the sunlight. Then a hiss and a rumble like thunder and Sojan and his companions were thrown to the floor. Still the rumble increased until blackness overcame them and they lost consciousness.

Sojan was the first to recover. Looking through the forward porthole he saw a sight which to him was terrifying. The velvet blackness of outer space, stars set like diamonds in its ebony beauty.

There was another rumble from the depths of the ship. With animal tenacity he sought to cling to consciousness. But it was no good. He collapsed once more on the floor of the ship.

He awoke a second time to see a blue sky above him and green vegetation beneath him. His friends rose on shaky legs.

"We're not much better off, it seems," grinned Sojan—cheerful now. "We're in the Poltoonian Wilderness. The nearest civilised land is Tigurn. See over there are the remains of a port similar to the one on the Shortani plain."

He pulled another lever. Immediately the portholes disappeared and they had the sensation of moving downwards at great velocity. A high pitched whine and they stopped. A panel slid open and a small bridge moved outwards over a drop of some five feet above the ground.

"There was probably a landing stage at this point," said Sojan with the air of an ancient professor delivering a lecture. "Anyway," he laughed, "we can drop the last few feet."

When they reached the ground they stood back.

Then the faint purr of machinery and the doors closed. Another sound, not quite so smooth—the chug-chug of an airship motor. The companions turned and saw several large airships of standard pattern circling above them. They flew the banner of Pelira, a country which had allegiance to Hatnor. Flying low, the captain of the airship inspected them, saw that they were not the strange monsters he had expected and landed his craft lightly fifty feet away from them. They ran towards it.

The look of astonishment on the captain's face was ludicrous. He immediately recognised the companions who, since their conquest of the priest-rulers of Rhan had become national heroes.

"What—what—?" was all he could get out at first.

"How're you fixed for fuel, friend?" laughed Sojan.

"We—we've got a full tank, sir, but how . . . ?"

"Then head for Hatnor," grinned the adventurer. "We'll explain on the way."

11. The Sons of the Snake-God

"WHO SEEKS to set foot in Dhar-Im-Jak?"

A harsh voice rang across the harbour to the merchantman *Kintonian Trader*, which ran at anchor there.

The captain cupped his hands into a megaphone and roared back at the soldier.

"Sojan Shieldbearer, late of the court of Nornos Kad in Hatnor, mercenary swordsman! Seeking employment!"

"I've heard of him. Very well, we need good sword arms in Dhar-Im-Jak, tell him he may land!"

Traani, captain of the *Trader*, called down to Sojan who sat sprawled in his cabin.

"They say you can land, Sojan!"

"Right, I'll get my gear together."

Ten minutes later, a tall figure stepped on to the deck of the ship. His long fair hair was held back from his eyes by a fillet of metal, his dark blue eyes had a strange, humorous glint in them. Over a jerkin of green silk was flung a heavy cloak of yellow, his blue breeches were tucked into leather boots. Upon his back was slung a long and powerful air rifle, on his left arm he carried a round shield. From a belt around his waist were hung a long vilthor and a pistol holster. Sojan the Swordsman was looking for work.

Later that day, in an inn near the city centre, Sojan met the man to whom he had been directed when he had told the authorities of the harbour what kind of employment he was seeking.

"You're looking for employment in the ranks of the regular military, I hear? What qualifications do you have?" he said.

"I was commander of the Armies of Imperial Hatnor for nearly a year. In that time I succeeded in stopping a rising in Veronlam, a similar rising in Asno, I organised the Poltoonian barbarians when Nornos Kad was deposed and restored him to his throne. I and four others were instrumental in utterly destroying the would-be conquerors of Zylor—the Rhanian Theocracy. I have been involved in several minor border wars, but of late things have quietened down and I thought that I would try my luck somewhere else. I heard of the impending war between the city states of Dhar-Im-Jak and Forsh-Mai and decided that I would like to take part."

"I have heard of you, Sojan. Your remark about Rhan jogged my memory. I feel that you would be a great asset to us. We need more professional soldiers of your calibre. As you know, both Dhar-Im-Jak and Forsh-Mai have been on friendly terms for hundreds of years, neither of us had any use for regular armies. Then about a year ago this new religious cult took over the ruling of Forsh-Mai and quickly formed an army of soldiers, spies, troublemakers and all kinds of undercover men. It was only recently that our own spies brought us the news that, as we suspected, Forsh-Mai was preparing to march into Dhar-Im-Jak and take over our republic."

"Have you any idea when they intend to attack?"

"In two weeks time, no less, I'm sure."

"Then we must work fast. I would be grateful to know what kind of command you intend giving me?"

"I shall have to discuss that with my superiors. I will naturally let you know as soon as possible."

Edek rose, downed the last of his drink and, with a short nod, left the inn. Just as Sojan was rising, there came a scream from the alley outside. Sword out, he rushed for the door to see a girl struggling in the grip of several burly fighting men. They were obviously bent on kidnapping her and Sojan lost no time in engaging the nearest hirelng. The man was an expert swordsman, his thrusts were well timed and it was all Sojan could do, at first, to parry them. The man's companions were still holding the girl who seemed to be making no attempt to get free. The clash of steel was music to him and a grim fighting smile appeared on his lips. Suddenly he felt a hard blow on the back of his head and the lights went out.

He regained consciousness in a small room, barred on both door and windows. Standing over him were two men; one held a water jug in his hand with which he was dousing Sojan.

"So our hard-headed mercenary is at last awake, I see!" The tone was gloating. The man's face did not belie the impression his voice gave. His thick black locks and beard were curled and oiled.

Upon his fingers were heavy rings, his nails were tinted with gold. Sojan looked at him in disgust. The bejewelled fop signalled to his companion to throw some more water at Sojan. Instantly Sojan rose and knocked the jug flying across the small cell.

"If your manners were as fine as the silks you wear, my friend, I should take you for *some* sort of man!"

The fop's face twisted for a moment and he half raised his hand. Then he smiled and dropped the hand to his side.

"We'll allow the wolf some time in which to cool the heat of his temper as water seems to be no use," he murmured. "Come Yuckof, let us leave this place—it smells!"

Sojan signalled to the guard who was locking the door.

"What place is this, friend?"

"You're in the Castle of Yerjhi, swordsman, we caught you nicely didn't we? That ruse in getting a girl to pretend that she was being captured was Lord Yerjhi's idea. He's a clever one. You'd be better off to be a little more civil to him, he is thinking of employing you."

Several hours later, Yerjhi returned with the same escort.

"Now, Sojan," he smiled, "I can understand your annoyance at being locked up in this place—but it was the only way in which we could—um—convince you of our sincerity when we offer you fifty thousand *derkas* to take command of our armies and lead them to glorious victory for the State of Forsh-Mai. We, the Sons of the Snake, will conquer all. Everything will be yours. What say you man, is that not a fair proposition?"

"Aye, it's fair," Sojan's eyes narrowed. He decided to bluff for a while. "*Fifty* thousand you say?"

"That and any spoils you can take for yourself when we loot Dhar-Im-Jak!"

"But what's this 'Sons of the Snake' you mention? Do I have to join some secret society to wield a sword for fifty thousand derkas?"

"That is a necessary part of our offer, Sojan. We are, after all, doing this for the glory of Rij, the Snake, Lord of the World and the After World, Master of Darkness, Ruler of the . . ."

"Yes, yes, we'll forget that for a moment. What does it involve?"

"First a meeting of all the major disciples, myself, the General-in-Command (who will take orders from you while the conquest is in progress), my majordomo, the two priests who invent—hmm—who spread the Truth of the Snake."

"But why this mumbo-jumbo—if you want to conquer your enemy, why not just do it? I can't understand what you're trying to do."

"Then briefly I will explain. The two cities have been at peace for hundreds of years. Men and women from the states have intermingled with each other, intermarried. Apart from the names and boundaries, we are practically the same people. We need an excuse, man, don't you see? We can't send a man to march against his brother or even son unless he thinks that there is something worth fighting for. This, my dear Sojan, is a—hmm—Holy war. Quite legitimate. We are—how shall I put it?—spreading the Word of the Snake God with the Sword of Justice! Part of our indoctrination campaign, actually, that last bit."

"Right! I'll join." Sojan had hit on a daring plan. "When do I become an initiate?"

An hour later, Sojan stood in a darkened room. In

front of him was a long table and at it sat men clad in robes decorated with serpents.

"Let the ceremony begin," he intoned.

Now was the time to act. They had given Sojan back his sword along with his other equipment and he now drew it. With the blade humming he downed the two nearest men. Three left, three wary men and led by one who had been described as the finest swordsman in Shortani.

Luckily only two of the men were swordsmen— the other was almost helpless. In the fore Yerjhi, cowl flung back and his face a mask of hate.

"Trick me would you," he hissed. "We'll show you what we do to dogs who try to turn on Yerjhi!"

Sojan felt a lancing pain go through him and he felt the warm blood as it trickled down his left arm. With renewed energy he launched himself at Yerjhi who was taken off guard for a moment. Clean steel pierced a tainted heart and the man toppled backwards with a short death-scream.

With the fake "Sons of the Snake God" exposed for what they were, what amounted to civil war was averted and the two cities resumed their friendly relations. Once again Sojan had done a major service for a cause in which he believed.

12. The Devil Hunters of Norj

THE LAST rays of Zylor's second sun were just waning when Sojan reined his myat and stared down into the green valley below.

He glanced at the crude map before him.

"This must be the Valley of Norj. It seems to be unexplored according to the map. Strange that no one has ventured into it."

Strange it was; for, even in the dusk, Sojan could see that the valley was lush and green. A river wound through it and brightly plumed birds sang from the branches of tall trees. A seeming paradise.

"It will make an excellent place to camp," thought the mercenary as he guided his mount downwards.

Later that night, he made his camp in a small natural clearing in the forest. His myat was tethered nearby and his campfire glowed cheerily. The night was warm and full of forest smells.

After eating his meal, Sojan climbed between his blankets and was soon asleep.

It was just after midnight when the strange noises awakened the warrior.

There they were again—a peculiar hissing screech

186

and the pounding of hooves; the cries of—men, and the vicious cracks of whips.

Sojan raised himself on one elbow, hand reaching for his sword. The myat stirred uneasily and swished its great tail from side to side.

The noises drew nearer and then subsided as they fell away towards the West of the valley.

Sojan did not sleep any more that night but kept a watchful eye open. The rest of the night was un-eventful and in the morning, Sojan cooked himself a big meal which was meant to last him the day, for he intended to investigate the noises he had heard the night before.

Riding slowly, with eyes always scanning the ground, Sojan soon found the tracks that the inhabitants of the valley had made. There were two distinct sets of tracks. One similar to those of a myat although with subtle differences, seemingly lighter. The others were entirely unfamiliar. Three-toed tracks like, and yet unlike, those of a bird—and considerably larger. The beast that had made them as obviously a quadruped of some kind, but other than that Sojan could not tell what kind of animal had made them—there were fourlegged birds he could think of—and none of these he had heard about were as large as this.

There had been at least ten riders, and it seemed that they had been chasing one or perhaps two of these bird-beasts. Probably some kind of hunt, thought Sojan, yet what kind of men were they who hunted at the dead of night?

Sojan rode on, following the tracks in the hope that he would find some clue to the mystery. He came across a steep inclination, the tracks ended here in a flurry of mud and—blood. Then the tracks of the beasts the men had been riding continued, and they had ridden for a short while parallel with the bluff and then forced their animals to ride up it.

Sojan did the same, the beast slipped occasionally and nearly slid back but eventually it reached the top. From there Sojan saw a strange scene.

A battle of some kind was going on between two groups of men. Near a squat black-stoned tower, five men, one mounted, were endeavouring to check a horde of armoured warriors who rushed from the tower. Beasts similar to Sojan's myat but hornless and almost tailless stood waiting.

The mounted man held the tethering reins of the other four animals while he cut at two of the armoured men with a battleaxe held in his right hand.

Although the mounted man was clad in armour, the other four were dressed only in jerkins of coloured cloth and divided kilts of leather. They were unshod and carried no sheaths for the weapons, mainly swords, with which they defended themselves. It seemed to Sojan that they were attempting to escape from the armoured warriors, one of whom, dressed more richly, and darker than the other, stood in the rear and urged them on in a language which was unfamiliar, yet strangely familiar, to Sojan's ears.

But there was no time to ponder over this now; the men needed help and Sojan, in a more curious than chivalrous mood, intended to aid them and perhaps find some answer to the mystery.

His long spear was out, his shield up and he forced the myat into a wild gallop down the hill, screaming to his gods in a barbarian war-shout.

His savage thrust caught the first of the armoured warriors in the throat and stayed there, the spear jerking like a tufted reed in a storm. His sword screamed from its scabbard as he pushed deeper into the mélée of cursing men.

Taking this chance of escape while the enemy were still confused, the other men quickly mounted their beasts. Sojan was still in the thick of it, sword lashing everywhere and dealing death with every stroke. One of the riders looked back, saw the mercenary still engaged and spurred his own beast back to where Sojan fought.

Grinning his thanks to Sojan he covered the mercenary's retreat with his own slim blade then followed.

Howling, the warriors attempted to pursue on foot, were brought back by their leader's frantic cries and scrambled round the back of the building.

The armoured rider called to Sojan in the familar, yet unintelligible tongue, and pointed towards the East. Sojan understood and turned his myat in that direction. Behind them their pursuers were whipping their steeds in an effort to overtake them.

Deep into the forest they rode, leaving their enemies far behind. For perhaps three hours they detoured until they reached the end of the valley where a sheer cliff rose. Brushing aside some shrubbery, the armoured man disclosed an opening in the base of the cliff.

Ducking their heads, the six rode through, the last man replacing the camouflage.

The passage ended in several connecting caves and it was in one of these that they stabled their mounts and continued on foot to the cave at the far end. Here they slumped into chairs, grinning with relief at their escape.

The leader, the man in armour began to speak to

Sojan who stood bewilderedly trying to understand the language in which they questioned him. Vaguely he began to realise what it was—it was his own tongue, yet so altered as to be scarcely recognisable. In an hour he could understand most of their speech and in two he was telling them how he had come to the Valley of Norj.

"But I am curious to find out who you are—and why men hunt giant four-legged birds at midnight," he said. "Who were the men from whom you escaped?"

"It is a long story to explain in a few words," said Jarg, the leader, "but I will first attempt to tell you a little of the political situation here, in Norj.

"There are two distinct races living here—men like ourselves—and—another race whom I scarcely like to define as 'men'. Ages ago our people reached this valley after a long sea voyage and trek across Shortani. we came to this valley and settled in it and it was not for some time that we learned that another people lived at the far end of the valley. A race of grim, blackhaired and black-eyed men, who hunted at night with steeltipped flails and who remained in their castles during the day. They did not trouble us at first and eventually we became used to the hunts, even though they sometimes passed through our fields and destroyed our crops. We were secure, we thought, in the valley and there was no man curious enough to venture too near the black-stoned castles of the Cergii.

"But soon men and women—even children—of our people began to disappear and the hunts became more frequent for the Cergii had found a new sport—a different quarry to the Devil-birds which they breed and release at night to hunt with their whips. It was then that the mangled bodies of our tribesmen began to be found—lashed to death.

"They were capturing our people—and hunting them! So it was that we declared war upon these beasts, these whom we had never harmed nor attempted to harm.

"Over the years traitors to our race went over to the enemy and became their warriors—you saw some of them today—our once great race dwindled—and became fugitives, living in caves and—if captured—the quarry of the Hunters of Norj. Still we carry on warfare with them—but it is hit and run fighting at best. The four you see here were captured recently and it was more by luck than anything that I managed to bribe a guard to release them. I came last night with weapons and myats—you see that the breed had changed as has our speech. Unfortunately the timing was imperfect and the first sun arose before we could make good our escape. We were seen and would all be dead or captured had it not been for you."

"There must be some way to defeat them!" cried Sojan. "And if there is a way—I swear that I will find it!"

Sojan and the fighting men of Norj, some sixty in all, stood in the main cave, waiting for nightfall.

Plans of Sojan's attempt to overcome the Cergii, who hunted men with steel-tipped flails, had been discussed and Sojan and Jarg, the leader, had reached a decision.

The Cergii were few, it seemed, about ten in number. They were immortal, or at least their life-spans

were incredibly long and the race had gradually dwindled to ten evil sorcerer-warriors whose only pleasure was the midnight hunts.

At dusk, Sojan rose, went over the final plan with
his friends, and left, heading Eastwards towards the
castles of the Cergii—some twenty in all, mostly in
an advanced state of decay—only one which housed
the Cergii and their Norjian slaves and hirelings.

The tiny Zylorian moons gave scant light and Sojan
found it difficult picking his way through the rubble
of the ruined outbuildings.

There came a faint scuffling behind him; a sound
which only a barbarian's senses could have heard.

Sojan ignored it and carried on.

Even when the scuffling came nearer he ignored
it. The sudden blow on the back of his head was
impossible to ignore, however, and a blind sense of
survival set him wheeling round, hand groping for
his sword hilt before blackness, deeper than night
swam in front of his eyes and he lost consciousness.

He awoke in a damp-smelling cell, only lit by
torchlight which filtered through a tiny grille in the
wall. The cell was obviously on a corner for the large
barred door was not in the same wall as the grille.

Peering through this door was an unkempt warrior clad in dirty armour and holding a spear.

He glared short-sightedly at the mercenary with
half-mad eyes. His mouth gaped pen showing bad
teeth and he chuckled loudly.

"You're the next game for the Hunters of Cergii,"
he cackled. "Oh! What a feast the beasts will have
tonight."

Sojan ignored these words, turned over and attempted to ease the pain in his aching head.

After many hours in which he attempted to get

some rest, Sojan was jabbed roughly awake by the guard's spear butt.

"What is it now?" he enquired as he raised himself to his feet and dusted off the straw in which he'd been sleeping.

"Heh, heh!" cackled the man. "It's almost midnight—time for one of our little hunts!"

Sojan became tense. He had a plan based on the knowledge that if he was captured he would most certainly be forced to partake in one of the hunts of the Cergii—as the quarry.

"Very well," he said, trying to sound as frightened as possible.

The courtyard was dark and gloomy, one moon showing through a gap in the ruins. The strange smell of an unknown animal came to Sojan's nostrils and he gathered that these were the "hounds" of the Cergii that Jarg had told him about.

He heard the stamping of the myats' hooves and the jingle of harness and, as his eyes became accustomed to the darkness, made out the vague outlines of tall mounted men.

"Is the quarry ready?" called out a voice as dead and cold as the ruins around them.

"Yes, Master, he is here!"

"Then tell him that he will be given quarter of an hour's start—then we will be upon his scent!" the voice went on.

The guards stood aside and Sojan was off—along a route already planned nights ago. His plan was a daring one and one which called for a great deal of courage. He was acting as a human snare for the Hunters.

Down a narrow forest trail he ran, the trees and grasses rustling in the cold night breeze, the sound of small animals calling to each other and the occasional scream as a larger animal made its kill.

The air in his lungs seemed to force itself out as he ran faster and faster. The time was getting short and he had several more minutes yet until he could reach the agreed spot.

Sounds—not the sounds of the forest, but more ominous—began to reach his ears. The sounds of cracking whips and thundering hooves as the Hunters and their silent hounds rode in pursuit.

Faster and faster he ran keeping his eyes open for the landmark which would afford him comparative safety.

At last it came into sight, just as the cracking of whips and pounding hooves seemed to be on top of him. Past the tall rock he ran, into a tiny gorge flanked on each side by towering rock walls.

Up the side of the cliff he scrambled as the Hunters entered the gorge. Then:

"Now!" roared Sojan, and as he did so sixty death-tipped arrows flew down and buried themselves in the bodies of many of the Cergii.

Their curses and frantic screams were music to Sojan and his friends as they fitted new arrows and let fly at the sounds.

Sojan leapt down the rocks again, a long sword in his right hand.

A shadowy rider loomed out of the darkness and an evil face, white teeth flashing in a grin of triumph, aimed a blow at Sojan with his own blade.

Sojan cut upwards, catching the rider in the leg. He screamed and tumbled off his steed, putting it between himself and Sojan.

He came upright, limping rapidly in the mercenary's direction. Sojan ducked another savage cut and parried it. Down lunged his opponent's sword attempting to wound Sojan's sword-arm. He again parried the stroke and counterthrust towards the man's chest.

Following up this move with a thrust to the heart, the mercenary ended the evil hunter's life.

Most of the Cergii were now either dead or mortally wounded and it did not take Sojan and his friends long to finish off the job they had started.

"Now for their hirelings!" yelled Sojan, goading his myat in the direction from which they had come; his sword dripping red in the moonlight, his hair tousled and a wildness in his eyes.

The sixty riders thundered down the narrow forest trail towards the castles of the dead Cergii, Sojan at their head, voicing a battle-cry which had been shouted at a dozen great victories for the men whom Sojan had led.

Straight into the courtyard they swarmed, catching the soldiers entirely unawares.

Dismounting, they crashed open the doors of the castle and poured in.

"Guard the doors!" yelled Sojan. "And all other exits—we'll exterminate every traitor in the place!"

His first call was in the dungeons—for there he knew he would find the man who had been his jailer during the previous day.

The half-crazed warrior cringed when he saw Sojan enter sword in hand. But one look at the tall mercenary told him that he could expect no mercy.

Drooling with fear he yanked his own sword from its scabbard and swung a blow at Sojan which would have cut him in two had it not been deflected by Sojan's blade.

Coolly Sojan fought while his opponent became more and more desperate.

Slowly the warrior was forced back as Sojan's relentless sword drove him nearer and nearer the wall.

His madness gave him immense stamina and gradually he began to fight with more skill.

"Heh, heh!" he cackled, "you will soon die man! Think not that you escaped death when you escaped the Cergii!"

Sojan smiled a grim smile and said nothing.

Suddenly the maddened warrior wrenched a spear from the wall and hurled it at Sojan. It plunked heavily into his left arm causing him to gasp with pain.

Then his eyes hardened and the warrior read his fate in them.

"You'll die for that," said Sojan calmly.

Almost immediately the warrior went down before a blurring network of steel and died with an inch of steel in his throat.

Sojan returned to the main hall of the castle where his friends were finishing off the rest of the Cergii's warriors.

"Well," he laughed cheerfully, "I must be off!"

Jarg turned. He saw the wound inflicted by the madman's spear.

"You can't ride in that state, Sojan!" he cried.

"Oh it will heal," Sojan smiled. "It is only a superficial cut! But you have work to do, restoring your farms now that the Cergii are vanquished. I should like to stay—but this is an interesting continent with lots to see. If I hurry I might be able to see it all before I die!"

With that he strode fom the room, mounted his

myat and cantered off, up the steep track which led out of the valley of Norj.

"There goes a brave man!" murmured Jarg as he watched him disappear over the hill-top.

JERRY CORNELIUS
AND CO.

New Worlds—
Jerry Cornelius

NEW WORLDS began as a magazine founded by SF enthusiasts in the middle 1940s. A consortium published the first few issues. This consortium consisted of, among others, Bill Temple, Ted Carnell, Leslie Flood, John Wyndham, Frank Arnold and Steve Frances. Later Maclarens took it over (though the company remained independent as Nova Publications Ltd.), and published it for the best part of its career with Ted Carnell as editor. Ted published the first Ballard stories and the work of then-starting authors like Brunner, Aldiss, Roberts, etc. In 1964 the circulations of the magazines (*Science Fantasy* was also edited by Ted) were very low and Maclarens decided to fold the titles. David Warburton of Roberts and Vinter Ltd., heard they were folding and decided to buy them. Ted wanted to edit his new anthology series, *New Writings in SF*, and so recommended me as editor. Warburton wanted two editors (wisely), one for each of the magazines. I chose *New Worlds* and Kyril Bonfiglioli became editor of *Science Fantasy*. My first issue, in a paperback-style format, but a magazine in all other respects, appeared for May-

June 1964 (number 142). We ran as a bi-monthly for a short time and then went monthly with issue 146. Many people expected me to opt for the editorship of *Science Fantasy*, since most of my work had previously appeared in that magazine, but in fact I was interested in broadening the possibilities of the SF idiom and *New Worlds*, being a much more open title, seemed the best place to do it. My first editorial stated pretty much the policy I have followed ever since, though perhaps I'm a little more sophisticated now. Also I was naïve in thinking there were a lot of authors who shared the sense of frustration which Ballard and I had felt for some years. I tried to find good young authors and follow what one might call a policy of enlightened conservatism—publishing the best of the old and the best of the new. There were a lot of outcries when we started dealing with explicit sex (never an important issue to us) and so on, also when the first Ballard fragmented narratives began to appear with *The Atrocity Exhibition*, also with the rather astringent criticism of "Golden Age" masters of SF, etc., but gradually readers began to realise that there was value in the new stuff and it didn't take long before they were criticising the newer stuff in its own terms. We *were* crusading but we weren't thinking in terms of tabu-breaking and so on, because the restrictions here had never been as marked as they were in the US. We were seriously attempting to find new ways of dealing with new subject matter and we always placed substance before style. People have since confused our "revolution" with a stylistic revolution, but our principal aim was concerned with substance and structure—it had little to do with what Judy Merril and Harlan Ellison, for instance, later came to term the "new wave" in US

SF. We were specifically out to perpetuate, if you like, the European moral tradition in literature. We hardly "rejected" the US pulp tradition, because it had never much influenced us anyway. Some of the writers, indeed, were quite conservative in their tastes and styles—Disch, for instance, who became closely associated with the magazine (and still is). While having no prejudice against it (and admiring much of it) we had little in common with the aims apparently represented in the work of the newer (or regenerated) US writers like Ellison, Delany, Zelazny, Lafferty or Silverberg. We also, of course, published most of those writers at some stage, and were pleased to do so, because we always strove for a broad representation of the best work of its kind. I feel we published some of the best work done by them— Zelazny's *For A Breath I Tarry* (later reprinted, I think, in *Amazing)* and several others: Ellison's *Boy and His Dog,* Delany's *Time Considered as a Helix,* etc. But our main *raison d'être* became the publishing of what some would call "experimental" work and when, in 1967, Roberts and Vinter suffered severe financial set-backs (not over the SF magazines), Brian Aldiss was responsible for suggesting to the Arts Council (responsible for encouraging and maintaining the arts; a government-financed agency) that they help us. Thanks largely to the enthusiasm of Angus Wilson, then chairman of the Council, and letters from various distinguished critics and academics (rallied by Brian) we received an award which, while not enough to support us in any way—save as a "little magazine"—gave us the moral support we needed and I became part-publisher, putting my own money into the magazine and going to the large, "glossy" format we then adopted. Unfortunately the two business partners I had to begin with showed themselves over-cautious and pulled out so that the magazine schedules were thrown into confusion. During 1967-8 we followed an erratic schedule culminating in the banning of two issues by the two major British distributors and the banning of the magazine in South Africa, New Zealand, Australia, etc. All of these areas were fairly crucial to us and if it hadn't been for advertising we should have had to fold. Also the newspapers came out in our favour and the ban was technically lifted. It was at this time that a Question was asked in the House of Commons about public money being spent on a "pornographic" magazine and it seemed for a while that we would lose the grant. This blew over and I became sole publisher of the magazine. Foolishly, I didn't form a company to publish the magazine, so that I became personally responsible for the debts. From 1968 to 1971 I published *New Worlds.* In 1970 it emerged that the distributors had been receiving large quantities of *New Worlds* and had deliberately refrained from distributing them without telling us because they wanted to avoid any further newspaper publicity. Effectively we lost the income on six months' issues and I suddenly found myself owing over £3000, which I didn't have. This was at a time when, thanks particularly to Charles Platt who was editing the magazine and running the business affairs, *New Worlds* had become viable. I was forced to wind *New Worlds* up, publishing a last "Subscription Only" issue (No. 201) in 1971, as an independent company. Tom Dardis of Berkley expressed an interest in doing *New Worlds* as a Quarterly and Anthony Cheetham was very enthusiastic about doing it through Sphere in this country, so I did four issues for Berkley who then decided that sales didn't merit their continuing the series. I decided, though the Sphere sales were on the increase, to cut back to two issues a year for the time being, since the Sphere advance alone wasn't sufficient to cover what I wanted to do and we're still partially financing the British editions through subsidiary income derived, for instance, from my editing fees for the *Best of New Worlds* series and so on. And, of course, I'm still paying off the creditors for the large size issues.

The daily routine? It varied, depending on who was publishing the magazine or, for that matter, who was editing it, since I didn't, of course, edit it for the whole time. The early days were fairly quiet, with just Lang Jones and myself doing the whole thing from an office I had in Southwark. Later I began to work from home, going into the publisher's office about once a week, and later still Charles Platt joined the staff as art editor and much improved the appearance of the paperback size issues. That period, too, was the only time I was actually getting paid to do it! By and large I tend to set one or two days aside for reading. Lang Jones is our best copy-editor and he would tend to do that (and still does) after I'd done the rough copy-editing. We never change stories without consultation with the author and the author's viewpoint is always respected. Where we have changes to suggest we tend to Xerox the manuscript, make the suggestions on the Xerox and send them to the author for his or her comments. If the author disagrees we'll discuss alternatives until we're both satisfied. This extends even to titles. The office always ran on democratic lines, with every editor being encouraged to encourage authors who suited his particular taste. This meant, of course, that I'd sometimes publish stories I couldn't stand or that I would include stories others didn't like, but we reached a fairly satisfactory compromise ("I'll put this story in I think is brilliant because you're putting in that story *you* think is brilliant.") I don't believe there's such a thing as objective literary judgement for someone running a magazine and it seemed the best way of ensuring the representation of as many different kinds of writing as possible. The special "New Writers" issues we have done have largely been the work of people like Jim Sallis, Graham Hall, Mike Harrison, Graham Charnock and Charles Platt. Through most of the magazine's career there was always something of a "commune" feel about the day-to-day editing, with authors and staff getting together to discuss specific stories or general policy. The issues about which I am happiest, I suppose, are the first few of the 1967-8 large size issues where my own policies found their strongest expression. To me, these were the best issues— say from 173 to 176 where we got a good balance between science and art features, artwork, good "conventional" fiction and good "experimental" fiction. Particular issues came after that which I particularly liked but not as a "run." I enjoyed doing the special 201st issue (labelled our Special Good Taste Issue and containing a distinctly Victorian feel!). The last thing I can think of to say about the day-to-day running of the magazine was that it filled the minds of a fairly large group of us for a long time—i.e. social life for many of us was centred around the magazine. It dominated our days. A rather heady and hectic love affair in which the magazine could be seen from time to time as either an inspiring mistress or a vampiric femme fatale. Certainly the publishing problems dominated my days and nights for several years.

I think we accomplished a fair amount. Without doubt we altered the attitudes of many publishers towards the newer ideas we were promoting. We encouraged many authors to do their best and/or most interesting work. Many authors, for instance, claimed that without *New Worlds* they would have given up writing or that they would have become cynical about their writing or that they wouldn't have put so much work into something. Aldiss, Ballard, Disch, Sladek, Roberts and others have all said, at different times, that *New Worlds* encouraged them to do their best work. We were responsible for interesting many critics, academics and journalists in what might be called the SF renaissance. I think we achieved an enormous amount. If what we were trying to do has been misinterpreted in America this has largely been because most people received their impressions at second-hand through, say, the Judith Merril *Year's Best* and *England Swings* anthologies. Judy did a lot to publicise *New Worlds* and was a good friend, but her interpretations were often somewhat at odds with our views! *New Worlds* became a banner in Judy's own crusade—and Judy, after all, started the ball rolling in the US. If the issues became clouded in rhetoric about "new wave speculative fiction" or "The New Thing', it wasn't much to do with us. Harlan Ellison followed Judy with *Dangerous Visions* and I think it's fair to claim that again, if obliquely, *New Worlds* supplied the impetus. I think, however, that battles are being fought in the States which have been over in this country for some years— everyone's settled down to doing their own thing. There was never any danger of one idea superceding another but it was necessary to make room for other ideas and that, if nothing else, is what *New Worlds* achieved. And our influence, if that isn't too pompous a phrase, extended well beyond the SF world in this country, if nowhere else. We know many rock musicians who've claimed that *New Worlds* gave them the impetus they were looking for, for we know artists, non-SF writers and poets who think the same. A lot of our ideas—and, indeed, our contributors—turned up in the pages of the "alternative" press. We still meet readers of the large size *New Worlds* who tell us it was the only magazine which gave them any hope or spoke to them in a vocabulary which made sense to them. And we have possibly influenced the vocabulary (both in terms of ideas and language) of SF–broadened its possibilities. Failures? We claimed too much for what we were doing in the early days and are only now beginning to see the results. We never licked the distribution problem—until it was too late—and so never reached as many readers as we might have done. We failed completely to convince the majority of fans that we felt writers like Heinlein were short-changing them with bad writing and simple-minded notions. We failed to improve the standard of writing in SF, which, in the main, remains abominable. On the other hand we offered an alternative to readers who couldn't face that kind of writing and, of course, we still do. We've certainly failed to convince the majority of US publishers concerning the merits of typical *New Worlds* fiction for they plainly prefer to publish the sensationalistic and poorly-conceived SF they have always published—and their preference doesn't appear to be dictated by commercial reasoning. We've failed, perhaps, to produce a large market for the kind of fiction we like best, but we have produced a large enough one to make publishing that fiction a viable proposition (which it wasn't even five years ago). And, by and large, we've failed to get across to most SF fans the seriousness of our intentions, the purpose of our intentions. This again, perhaps, is because our particular point of view has been obscured by interpreters. Certainly *New Worlds'* policy has little to do with what most US fans would identify as the "SF New Wave".

Which, I suppose, almost brings us to Jerry Cornelius.

Jerry Cornelius began as a version of Elric of Melniboné when, in late 1964, I was casting around for a means of dealing with what I regarded as the "hot" subject matter of my own time—stuff associated with scientific advance, social change, the mythology of the mid-twentieth century. Since Elric was a "myth" character I decided to try to write his first stories in twentieth-century terms. *The Final Programme* was written, in first draft, in about ten days in January 1965. It began as a kind of rewrite of the first two Elric stories, *The Dreaming City* and *While the Gods Laugh*. By doing this I found a style and a form which most suited what I wanted to write about. I was elated. I borrowed as much from the Hammett school of thriller fiction as I borrowed from SF and I think I found my own "voice" as a writer. Influences included Ronald Firbank and, to a minor extent, William Burroughs (two not dissimilar figures in my estimation). I felt, at the time, that I had at last found a way of marrying "serious" fiction with "popular" fiction and I had always believed that science fiction was the form which could most easily act, as it were, as the ideal environment in which this marriage could take place. (This, incidentally, was the idea which was behind much of the *New Worlds* policy). SF knew how to cope with much of the subject matter and was a vital and popular form but was largely unable to deal with the traditional and sophisticated moral questions found in the best fiction, largely because its accepted forms had denied any attempt authors might make to incorporate these questions—the form as it stood distorted and simplified the problems. Just as Ballard found his remedy in the form he used for *Atrocity Exhibition* and the later stories published from 1965 onwards, I felt I'd found my remedy in the form I used in *The Final Programme*—by using a character who *accepted* the moral questions without discussing them (the dialogue tends to take for granted the reader's familiarity with the questions and doesn't detail them—doesn't spell them out) and by supplying the reader with a straightforward dynamic narrative which he could enjoy for its own sake. The plot, while being unimportant, was supplied for those who required a plot to keep them reading. Morever, I prefer, in the main, books with a straightforward plot, too, so I was trying to produce something I'd enjoy reading. I was very pleased with the book and thought that everyone else would enjoy it, too, if only for its ironies and sensations. A couple of British publishers asked to see it and surprised me with their strong reactions—I'd written the book to shock, they said, and I wouldn't get anywhere like that. It hadn't occurred to me that the book would do anything but amuse (if nothing else). I despaired, became cynical, put the book aside. A copy went out automatically to my, then, agents, Scott Meredith. In 1967 the book was bought, enthusiastically, by George Ernsberger, then an editor at Avon. Parts of it had been published in *New Worlds* in 1965 and 1966 as an experiment in cutting up chunks and putting them in a different order (a mistake, I now think). By this time I had begun what was eventually published as *A Cure For Cancer*. I had started the book using another character's name and hadn't got very far when I realised that this was effectively a sequel to the Jerry Cornelius novel. I put what I'd written aside and thought about it all, eventually conceiving the notion of writing a tetralogy of books about Jerry, each one expanding upon the various moral questions raised in *The Final Programme*. I visited New York in 1967 and told George Ernsberger about my scheme and George, was, again, enthusiastic. Eventually, in 1968, I had a contract from Avon for the remaining three books. By this time *The Final Programme* had been bought by Allison and Busby who were equally enthusiastic and had also bought *Behold the Man* in its novel version. They, too, were pleased with the tetralogy idea and guaranteed to publish them in England. It gave me the necessary encouragement to carry on with *A Cure For Cancer* which took, in all, some three years to write, appearing first as a serial in *New Worlds*. In 1968, *The Final Programme* was published, at the time when Jim Sallis had come over to work on *New Worlds*. Jim read the book and was very enthusiastic about it. When Lang Jones was commissioned to edit the big hardback anthology for Hutchinson, *The New SF*, he asked me for a story and I decided that I would try to write a Jerry Cornelius story (this was *The Peking Junction*)—developing some of the techniques I was beginning to feel happy with while working on *A Cure For Cancer*. Jim Sallis asked me, then, if I had any objection to his writing a Jerry Cornelius story since, in his opinion, the JC stories were a form in themselves. I had none, of course. He wrote *Jeremiad*, which was published in *New Worlds*. Taking up part of a theme I'd put into my second JC short, *The Delhi Division*, he expanded from there and wrote an entirely different story. Taking up part of his theme I wrote it back into *Delhi Division*, which he'd so far only seen in rough draft. *The Delhi Division* was the first JC short to appear in *New Worlds* and was quickly followed by *Jeremiad*. Once this had happened several others who had enjoyed *The Final Programme* felt that they'd like to do a story about Jerry, so shortly afterwards there appeared stories by Brian Aldiss, Norman Spinrad, a poem by Lang Jones, and other stories by M. John Harrison, Maxim Jakubowski and one other by me *The Tank Trapeze*. (Most of these were eventually published in a book called *The Nature of the Catastrophe* (Hutchinson, 1971). In the meantime I had also begun a comic strip for *It*, then the leading underground paper in Britain, with Mal Dean, who had illustrated many of the JC stories. The *It* strip sent up many of the current obsessions of the underground—the mysticism, the political naïvete and so on. We began to alternate, with Mike Harrison and Richard Glyn Jones taking up our themes and us taking up their themes turn by turn. The strip ran for about a year in *It* as *The Adventures of Jerry Cornelius, The English Assassin*. Part of the strip was also published in *The Nature of the Catastrophe*. In our terms we found a cool way of dealing with hot material. The essence of the stories is their irony, their attempts to concentrate as much information as possible into as small a space as possible, their obsession with contemporary imagery, their strong reliance on metaphorical imagery drawn from many disparate sources—pop music, astronomy, physics, cybernetics, etc. They are, ideally, deeply serious in intention. Unfortunately many critics have missed the serious points of the stories, even if they've found the stuff entertaining. Sexual ambiguity, for instance, is taken for granted in the JC stories—a fact of life—but critics continue to see that element, among others, as "daring". In this country, at any rate, the stories receive their most intelligent responses from that section of the public most at ease with what's these days called the "alternative' society, was earlier called "beat" and before that called "bohemian" —i.e. people who by and large do take certain things for granted which are regarded as shocking by the average middle-class person. I'm not here suggesting that this is good or bad, but it is a fact. Judy Merril, for instance, regarded *The Final Programme* as an "evil" book. Other people have expressed similar reactions. I find them almost impossible to understand. Perhaps people will get a better idea of the JC novels when the whole tetralogy is complete. *The English Assassin* will be out in England this year, after three years in the writing. I don't know when the last book, *The Condition of Muzak*, will appear— probably in a couple of years, maybe three or four. I'll just have to wait patiently until then. At present, while having reservations about the first two books, I'm very satisfied with *Assassin*—it's the first book of mine I've been able to proof-read without wincing all the way through. Presumably Holt Reinhardt, who did *Cure*, will be doing *Assassin* in the States sometime next year. I haven't had any information either from Avon or from Holt, as yet. Maybe *Final Programme* will get its points across better as a film.

The rights have been bought and the script written and it's being produced by the company who did *Performance* (which has something in common with *Final Programme*). I heard Jagger turned down the JC part as being too freaky and I don't know if the film ever will be made, but it would be interesting to see how the public reacted to it. I think the JC stories have matured considerably since *Final Programme*—becoming better written and more complex—and it *does* disappoint me when people don't enjoy them or find them obscure. I remember the delight I felt at producing a book which I was sure everyone would find at very least entertaining. I was puzzled when some people reacted in a puzzled or even antagonistic way. My own wavelengths changed somewhere at some time. These days, for instance, I can't understand SF—I read the words and they no longer mean anything to me, even when written by a writer I used to enjoy. So I suppose I can appreciate how people feel when they find a JC story they can't focus on. It isn't incidentally, anything to do with radical alterations in life-style on my part. It just happened at some point. Ho hum.

(Letter to reader)

In Lighter Vein

A Note on the Jerry Cornelius Tetralogy

PART of my original intention with the Jerry Cornelius stories was to "liberate" the narrative; to leave it open to the reader's interpretation as much as possible—to involve the reader in such a way as to bring his own imagination into play. The impulse was probably a result of my interest in Brecht—an interest I'd had since the mid-fifties.

Although the structure of the tetralogy is very strict (some might think over-mechanical) the scope for interpretation is hopefully much wider than of a conventional novel. The underlying logic is also very disciplined, particularly in the last three volumes. It's my view that a work of fiction should contain nothing which does not in some way contribute to the overall scheme. The whimsicalities to be found in all the books are, in fact, not random, not mere conceits, but make internal references. That is to say, while I strive for the effect of randomness on one level, the effect is achieved by a tightly controlled system of internal reference, puns, ironies, logicjumps which no single reader may fairly be expected to follow.

Thus, in a scene in *Condition of Muzak* (the end of the section called "Outcast of the Islands"), there is a short discussion about the Japanese invasion of Australia and Jerry makes a reference to big egoes and Hitler. Shakey Mo then asks if he was a character in a children's comic and then immediately asks if Hitler wasn't a police chief they'd met in Berlin. The first reference is to Big Ego (a cartoon ostrich in *The Dandy* or *The Beano*); the second reference is to an earlier story of mine (a "key" story, in my view) called *The Pleasure Garden of Felippe Sagittarius* (where Hitler was a rather pathetic police chief in an imaginary Berlin), leading to a reference to the fact that the historical Adolf Hitler doesn't exist in this world.

All this happens in a couple of sentences or so and should give the effect, among others, of time in a state of flux, men in a state of introverted confusion, close to fugue, and so on. But its internal logic is straightforward: the two characters know exactly what they are talking about. To "explain" all this, to editorialise, would be to break the mood, break the dramatic tensions, and ruin the effect I was trying to achieve. The apparent obscurity should not confuse the reader because the narrative should be moving so rapidly that he shouldn't care if he doesn't understand every reference. Similarly, if he was watching a richly textured film, he would not expect to perceive consciously every detail of every scene, dialogue, music, etc. They are maintained primarily by a complicated series of prefiguring images which are developed as the book progresses.

(*Note to bibliography*)

The Stone Thing
1975

A Tale of Strange Parts

OUT OF the dark places; out of the howling mists; out of the lands without sun; out of Ghonorea came tall Catharz, with the moody sword Oakslayer in his right hand, the cursed spear Bloodlicker in his left hand, the evil bow Deathsinger on his back together with his quiver of fearful rune-fletched arrows, Heartseeker, Goregreedy, Soulsnatcher, Orphanmaker, Eyeblinder, Sorrowsower, Beanslicer, and several others.

Where his right eye should have been there was a jewel of slumbering scarlet whose colour sometimes shifted to smouldering blue, and in the place of his left eye was a many-faceted crystal, which pulsed as if possessed of independent life. Where Catharz had once had a right hand, now a thing of iron, wood and carved amethyst sat upon his stump; nine-fingered, alien, cut by Catharz from the creature who had sliced off his own hand. Catharz' left hand was at first merely gauntleted, but when one looked further it could be observed that the gauntlet was in fact a many jointed limb of silver, gold and lapis lazuli, but as Catharz rode by, those who saw him pass remarked not on the murmuring sword in his right hand, not on the whispering spear in his left hand, not on the whining bow upon his back or the grumbling arrows in the quiver; neither did they remark on his right eye of slumbering scarlet, his left eye of pulsing crystal, his nine-fingered right hand, his shining metallic left hand; they saw only the fearful foot of Cwlwwymwn which throbbed in the stirrup at his mount's right flank.

The foot of the Aching God, Cwlwwymwn Root-ripper, whose ambition upon the old and weary Earth had been to make widows of all wives; Cwlw-wymwn the Striker, whose awful feet had trampled whole cities when men had first made cities; Cwlw-wymwn of the Last Ones, Last of the Last Ones, who had been driven back to his island domain on the edge of the world, beyond the Western Ice, and who now came limping after Catharz screaming out for vengeance, demanding the return of his foot, sliced from his leg by Oakslayer so that Catharz might walk again and continue upon his doomladen quest, bearing weapons which were not his protection but his burden, seeking consolation for the guilt which ate at his soul since it was he who had been responsible for the death of his younger brother, Forax the Golden, for the death of his niece, Libia Gentleknee, for the living death of his cousin, Wertigo the Unbalanced, seeking the whereabouts of his lost love, Cyphila the Fair, who had been stolen from him by his arch-enemy, the wizard To'me'ko'op'r, most powerful, most evil, most lustful of all the great sorcerers of this magic-clouded world.

And there were no friends here to give aid to

Catharz Godfoot. He must go alone, with shuddering terror before him and groaning guilt behind him,
and Cwlwwymwn, screaming, vengeful, limping
Cwlwwymwn, following always.

And Catharz rode on, rarely stopping, scarcely
ever dismounting, anxious to claim his own vengeance on the sorcerer, and the foot of Cwlwwymwn,
Last of the Last Ones, was heavy on him, as well it
might be for it was at least eighteen inches longer
than his left foot and naked, for he had had to
abandon his boot when he had found that it did not
fit. Now Cwlwwymwn possessed the boot; it was
how he had known that Catharz was the mortal who
had stolen his green, seventeen-clawed limb, attach-
ing it by fearful sorcery to the flesh of his leg. Catharz'
left leg was not of flesh at all, but of lacquered cork,
made for him by the People of the World Beneath
the Reefs, when he had aided them in their great
fight against the Gods of the Lowest Sea.

The sun had stained the sky a livid crimson and
had sunk below the horizon before Catharz would
allow himself a brief rest and it was just before dark
that he came in sight of a small stone cottage, sheltered beneath terraces of glistening limestone, where
he hoped he might find food, for he was very hungry.

Knocking upon the door he called out:

"Greetings, I come in friendship, seeking hospitality, for I am called Catharz the Melancholy, who
carries the curse of Cwlwwymwn Rootripper upon
him, who has many enemies and no friends, who
slew his brother, Forax the Golden, and caused the
death of Libia Gentleknee, famous for her beauty,
and who seeks his lost love Cyphila the Fair, prisoner of the wizard To'me'ko'op'r, and who has a
great and terrible doom upon him."

The door opened and a woman stood there. Her hair was the silver of a spiderweb in the moonlight, her eyes were the deep gold found at the centre of a beehive, her skin had the pale, blushing beauty of the tea-rose. "Welcome, stranger," said she. "Welcome to all that is left of the home of Lanoli, whose father was once the mightiest in these parts."

And, upon beholding her, Catharz forgot Cyphila the Fair, forgot that Cwlwwymwn Rootripper limped after him still, forgot that he had slain his brother, his niece, and betrayed his cousin, Wertigo the Unbalanced.

"You are very beautiful, Lanoli," he said.

"Ah," said she, "that is what I have learned. But beauty such as mine can only thrive if it is seen and it has been so long since anyone came to these lands."

"Let me help your beauty thrive," he said.

Food was forgotten, guilt was forgotten, fear was forgotten as Catharz divested himself of his sword, his spear, his bow and his arrows and walked slowly into the cottage. His gait was a rolling one, for he still bore the burden that was the foot of the Last of the Last Ones, and it took him some little time to pull it through the door, but at length he stood inside and had closed the door behind him and had taken her in his arms and had pressed his lips to hers.

"Oh, Catharz," she breathed. "Catharz!"

It was not long until they stood naked before one another. Her eyes travelled over his body and it was plain that the eyes of scarlet and crystal were lovely to her, that she admired his silver hand and his nine-fingered hand, that even the great foot of Cwlwwymwn was beautiful in her sight. But then her eyes, shy until now, fell upon that which lay between his legs, and those eyes widened a little, and she blushed. Her lovely lips framed a question, but he moved forward as swiftly as he could and embraced her again.

"How?" she murmured. "How, Catharz?"

"It is a long tale and a bloody one," he whispered, "of rivalry and revenge, but suffice to say that it ended in my father, Xympwell the Cruel, taking a terrible vengeance upon me. I fled from his court into the wastes of Grxiwynn, raving mad, and it was there that the tribesmen of Velox found me and took me to the wise Man of Oorps in the mountains beyond Katatonia. He nursed me and carved that for me. It took him two years, and all through those two years I remained raving, living off dust and dew and roots, as he lived. The engravings had mystical significance, the runes contain the sum of his great wisdom, the tiny pictures show all that there is to show of physical love. Is it not beautiful? More beautiful than that which it has replaced?"

Her glance was modest; she nodded slowly.

"It is indeed, very beautiful," she agreed. And then she looked up at him and he saw that tears glistened in her eyes. "But did it *have* to be made of Sandstone?"

"There is little else," he explained sadly, "in the mountains beyond Katatonia."

> (From *The Outcast of Kitzoprenia* Volume 67 in *The History of the Purple Poignard*)

DAW

Discover the Enchantment of
Michael Moorcock

Elric of Melniboné
ELRIC AT THE END OF TIME.
Come with the Prince of Melnibone as he ventures to the very
end of time itself, standing beside the immortals as Chaos
launches its last great assault on a crumbling universe.

(#UE2040—$2.95)

The Runestaff Series
Dorian Hawkmoon fell under the power of the Runestaff, a
mysterious artifact more ancient than time itself. Its spell shaped
a destiny that involved Hawkmoon in strange, destructive
schemes and in wild, uncanny adventures in distant places as
he battled to the death the evil forces of the Dark Empire that
threatened to betray his very heritage. The Runestaff novels
are among the great classics of fantastic adventure.

☐ **THE JEWEL IN THE SKULL**   (#UE2175—$2.95)

☐ **THE MAD GOD'S AMULET**   (#UE2216—$2.95)

☐ **THE SWORD OF THE DAWN**   (#UE2173—$2.95)

☐ **THE RUNESTAFF**   (#UE2218—$2.95)

DAW

DAW

SCIENCE FICTION MASTERWORKS FROM
THE INCOMPARABLE
C.J. CHERRYH